D0732604

Purchased from
Multnomah County Library
Title Wave Used Bookstore
216 NE Knott St, Portland, OR
503-988-5021

THE
HORSE LATITUDES

MATTHEW ROBINSON

PROPELLER BOOKS
P.O. Box 1238
Portland, OR 97207

This book is a work of fiction. Names, characters, places, and incidents either are products of the author's imagination or are used fictitiously. Any resemblance to actual events or locales or persons, living or dead, is entirely coincidental.

Copyright © 2016 Matthew Robinson

All rights reserved. No part of this book may be used or reproduced in any manner whatsoever without written permission from the publisher, except in the case of brief quotations embodied in critical articles or reviews. For further information, contact Propeller Books, P.O. Box 1238, Portland, OR 97207-1238.

First U.S. Edition 2016

Cover and interior design by Context

Published by Propeller Books, Portland, Oregon.
ISBN 978-0-9827704-5-0

Parts of this book previously appeared, sometimes in different form, in the following publications: "A Sleeping Tank in the Date Fields" in *Split Lip Magazine*; "First Sergeant Orders a Formation" in *Gobshite Quarterly*, Issue 15/16; "The Combo" in *Nailed Magazine*; "Sergeant Hicks Guards a Bomb" in *O-Dark-Thirty*, Vol. 4, No. 1; "V is for Valor" and "Sergeant Mills Watches a Fight" in *War Stories 2015: An Anthology* (Blue Skirt Press, 2015); "Baptism" in *Clackamas Literary Review*, Vol. XX.

www.propellerbooks.com

Printed in the United States of America

for Diesel,
Jaxon,
Kinhly,
and Lola

and for Justin, Justin, Erik, and David
who are already at the Green

CONTENTS

11   GARRISON ENVIRONMENT

21   POINT OF ORIGIN

29   COWBOYS

39   BLEEDER

49   STAFF SERGEANT HICKS GUARDS A BOMB

61   PEDESTRIANS

69   THE HORSE LATITUDES

75   STAFF SERGEANT HICKS TAKES A DRINK

85   BAPTISM

91   OBSERVATION POST

99   COUNSELOR

105   THE COMBO

111   OPSEC

123   COFFEE & BAKLAVA

133   V IS FOR VALOR

143   THE RIFLE

THE HORSE LATITUDES

O, why should nature build so foul a den,
Unless the gods delight in tragedies?

—Shakespeare, *Titus Andronicus*

An idea about Shakespeare.
That the play demands coming to the surface—hence insists
upon a reality which the novel need not have, but perhaps
should have contact with the surface, coming to the top.

—Virginia Woolf, *A Writer's Diary*

The dignity of movement of an iceberg is due to only one-
eighth of it being above water.

—Ernest Hemingway, *Death in the Afternoon*

Hemingway was a cunt.

—Private First Class Napes, Baghdad, Iraq, 2004

GARRISON ENVIRONMENT

"What's this about?" Specialist Gleeson said.

"No idea," Sergeant Mills said.

"It's probably going to be something super important."

"Oh, undoubtedly." The noon sun burned softly. Sweat clung but didn't run. Mills ground his boot tread into gravel until he felt settled, the rest of the company crunching around him.

The barracks door swung open and the First Sergeant walked out into the motor pool. The XO strolled out behind him and took a leaning position against the wall. He fished out a can of chewing tobacco from his blouse pocket. The First Sergeant took his place at the front of the company, index cards in hand. He shuffled through them. Mills thought it looked like his lips were moving a little for each one. Maybe some muttering. When he looked up his face was red from nerves or heat or both, and what Mills believed was a quiet, professional alcoholism.

"Form up," Top said. The eighty men, already grouped by platoon, shuffled into rank and file. Hot wind scattered kicked-up dust. "Men, we've been here for a month and the place already looks like shit. Trucks parked every which way, trash all over the goddamn place. You think you're in the Nam, but you're not. This is the Occupation—we're here for sustainment operations." The horizon sat behind him, columns of smoke rising up across the city. Fifty meters beyond the perimeter wall, cars passed over a length of elevated freeway, traffic petering out until the road was just one more thing sitting unused in Baghdad.

"We will unfuck this AO. Platoon sergeants have the duty rosters." He moved to the next card.

Mills hadn't slept or shaved in two days, since before the last mission. If he breathed deep enough, he could feel his collar catch on whiskers as he exhaled. He tried to lower his chin and shrug his shoulders up, shrink into his uniform, hide the scruff some. But it was too far—he gave up. His blouse rubbed sweat and grit into the hairs along his neck as he dropped his shoulders. The sensation was tender. He did it again.

"And uniforms. I see visible bracelets, hair over the ears, sideburns, porno-staches. Cut your fucking hair. Supply has shears and there's a Hajji barber over by the laundry. By the end of the day you will all be within regs and those bracelets will be off."

Gleeson raised his hand—a green braid tight on his wrist.

"What?" Top said.

Mills shrugged again, up fast, down slow. It was like being touched.

"My fiancée tied this on when we left," Gleeson said.

"We're cutting it off together when I get home." Someone in the formation said *Same*, real quiet. *Me too*, a little louder. *Bullshit*, loudest.

Gleeson smiled. He had worn his bracelet for three months and seven days—since the day he proposed. The teardrop-shaped scar from singeing off the cut cord ends was still red against his tan wrist.

Mills whispered out the side of his mouth, "You don't even love her. You just wanted your bitching to carry the additional weight of having dependants."

"If so, getting engaged on the way to war was the most soldierly thing I've ever done."

Past Top's head, out on the freeway, two vans stopped. Without turning, Mills eyed the road in both directions. There was nothing. He looked back to the First Sergeant.

"That's the sweetest goddamn thing I've ever heard," Top said. "Who's that, Gleeson? Fucking figures. Next time pick something you're allowed to wear. They come off or you get an Article 15." More muttering. "In fact," he patted the six-inch KA-BAR hanging from his belt, "we'll handle this immediately after formation."

Gleeson dropped his smile.

Mills dropped his shoulders and left them dropped.

One of the vans began unloading men. The first two shouldered AKs and pointed them in opposite directions, up and down the freeway. The third wore his rifle slung across his back. He said something over his shoulder but it died in the fifty meters of wind. Mills wondered if they were Iraqi police who had found an IED. The third man brought binoculars to his face, the glinting lenses scanning the FOB. *Not IPs*, Mills thought. The last man shouldered something as he stepped out of the van but stayed behind his spotter. The second van opened its side door, no one got out.

"Also, we are reinstituting the greeting of the day. If you pass an officer on this base, you will salute." Someone said *Bullshit* again. Others laugh-coughed. "We're professional soldiers. We're going to look and act like it. It's been a year, men, since the war ended. Remember? Big boat? Big sign? Mission fucking accomplished? America is established here—this is a garrison environment."

The XO stood dark and lean under the barracks overhang, shook his head—spit black chew at Top's shadow.

The open van flashed orange with a dull thud as an RPG slammed against the freeway railing, exploding into black smoke. The formation crouched and looked toward the sound. The backblast of a second RPG came from the four dismounts, orange and gray rising behind them, a rocket hissing toward the base.

"Incoming!" Men scattered on their bellies, behind trucks, toward the perimeter wall, into the barracks. Mills's fear pushed up from his guts, flashed across his face like a struck match head. His lips throbbed in time with his pulse as his hands went cold and shaky. He took steps in each direction, started for the ground, then back up—there was no battle drill for taking fire during formation. The rocket hit the empty helo-pad fifty meters past its intended target, extinguishing itself in concrete—a cloud of dust, and a soft *boom* sounded.

Gleeson came up on his knees, one hand fingering his bracelet, checking for frays, looking at the small dust cloud. Mills cupped his neck where his collar had rubbed. Top looked where his formation had been, then to the index cards in his hands. His cheeks were red and his fore-head was white.

"Mount up!" said the XO. He pulled the bulge of chew from his lip with a hooked finger, threw the dark wad at the First Sergeant.

Mills and Gleeson ran to their truck. As they approached Top, Gleeson saluted, yelling, "Afternoon, First Sergeant!" He dropped the salute. Running past, they smelled shit. It was coming off Top.

They secured their gear, Gleeson in the turret, Mills in the back seat. They waited for their driver and truck commander. "Can you fucking believe that?" Gleeson said.

"Not really," Mills said, sliding a magazine into his M-4. Locked the bolt to the rear. "Somebody fucked up. Only one of those rockets made it in. One van is still sitting there. Are you up?"

Gleeson slammed his feed tray cover closed. "Roger, I'm up. They fired from inside the van. We're rolling up on burnt Hajjis. I want to give Top the count myself."

"Silver lining? I don't think your bracelet is an issue anymore."

"Goddamn right. I at least have until he changes his fucking pants."

Private First Class Napes got into the driver's seat and started the truck. Staff Sergeant Hicks sat in the TC seat and said, "Move out."

Gleeson dug into his cargo pocket, pulled out something white and crinkling. As the truck drove past, he sent it sailing. The bag of baby wipes slapped up dust at Top's feet.

Outside the gate Mills let his bolt slam forward. He

snapped his dust cover closed and hit his forward assist three times with his palm. *Tick tick tick.* The collar of his vest gripped his neck. He shrugged his shoulders, sunk into it, but it just clung to him. He dropped his shoulders. The collar wouldn't let go.

Robinson,

I read your story. It's shit.

Stone

POINT OF ORIGIN

The desert is brown. The buildings are brown. The streets are brown. The sky is blue.

My uniform is three shades of brown. The eight million Iraqis who live here are a multitude of browns. The backs of my formerly pink hands are burnt brown. The sky is massively blue.

What I miss is green. Trees. Weeds. My uniform before this fucking war. Home is green. With a sky that's sometimes blue and sometimes gray and sometimes pink. This Baghdad sky is devoutly blue all day. Then growling red. Then dark-dark, when the fast is broken, all headlights and trash fires and muzzle flashes, embedded in black. Ramadan sky.

We are driving through neighborhoods, throwing candy to kids. Sometimes soccer balls with propaganda printed on them. I'm looking out the window of my truck, watching all the brown.

It's fucking hot.

Thunk. Thunk. Thunk.

The sound comes from all directions, having swept around buildings and the massive cemetery and through the underpass and up the goddamn riverbank. For the split second before impact, they each give a small scream. We see nothing.

Boom. Boom. Boom.

The explosions are beyond us, several blocks away, muffled by shop fronts and apartment buildings and traffic and people.

All four gunners on all four trucks duck into their hatches and yell, "Contact!" Four give the clock direction of the Point of Impact as two o'clock. Two mistakenly identify it as an IED. Two correctly identify it as mortar fire but disagree as to its Point of Origin. I don't believe either of them really knows where it came from. But then, I'm just sitting, looking out the window, waiting for us to turn onto the side roads and go chasing echoes. After some arguing over the radio, Sergeant First Class Kurtzson decides that his gunner is more correct than Sergeant Sawyer's and off we go.

Our four-lane, well-paved downtown street is too full of people. The buildings that hem us in are several stories tall, brutal in their top-heavy concrete facades, like inverted castles, with glass-windowed storefronts on the ground floor. The sidewalks are packed with vendors cooking meat on small, open-flame grills and in carts covered in steaming pots and bags of pita. Entire stores are laid out on unfurled rugs—reds and purples, vibrant even under the dust. The outermost lanes are overrun with pedestrians. The two center lanes are for driving but traffic is moving too slow. Our gunners begin flagging Iraqi drivers into the outer lanes with the barrels of their machine guns. We road march down the centerline to the nearest intersection. We turn onto two-lane dirty pavement, dead but for sporadic clusters of kids.

The commercial buildings taper off and two-story residences begin to fill my window. Upper-level windows are taped over with large brown Xs. Courtyards begin to overflow with potted plants. I just want to pull over, occupy one corner of one courtyard, and feel plant leaves between my fingers. But we keep driving. There are no people out. It's midday and I'm sweat-soaked. I drag a finger across my sleeve, tracing a salt stain.

I lean forward and look between Gleeson's legs and Napes's Kevlar. I'm in the back seat. Through the windshield, past the two middle trucks, our lead truck turns onto an unpaved road. Beyond it is all green. And the blue above it. As we make the turn, outside my window is a date field that goes on forever. Trees and grass. Dirt a color so different than sand, I don't even hate that it's brown.

Thunk thunk thunk.

"Contact!" Gleeson yells down. And softly, a long way off, *boom boom boom.* I want out. I want my boots off. I want to stand in the tall grass and squish my toes in soil. Our trucks speed up and begin turning onto narrow, unpaved paths, built up across the fields, irrigation ditches running alongside. Top-heavy and husky-trunked date trees block most of the view. It's goddamn beautiful. They run in lines, breaking the field into a grid, but the lines aren't straight. They meander as my eyes track them.

The radio is loud with conflicting reports of distance and direction, where they think the POO is. I realize that we are possibly approaching bad guys. I hit the forward assist of my M-4 with my palm. Sometimes all you can do is repeatedly ensure your first round is fully seated. It makes a small: *tick tick tick.*

The green goes by.

The radio opens up: "Contact! Tank! Three o'clock!"

It's several hundred meters away, but it's directly in my line of sight. I should have seen it before I heard about it. I don't think I'm much good at this.

Our trucks stop. The radio says, "Dismounts out."

I tap the forward assist twice, take my rifle to the low-ready, pointed at the tank but forty-five degrees toward the ground, and I move off the hard-packed dirt of the road into the green field. Inside my boots I squish my toes into my socks. It almost feels right. I pull a piece of grass loose. I squeeze. All along the row of trucks, one dismount from each moves onto the field. We halt, make sure we are on-line. The tank used to be brown, but is rusting red. The green has grown half way up it, and its barrel is gone—removed and repurposed. I relax some, before I remember that something went *thunk.* I let go of my piece of grass. *Tick tick tick.* I scan the field. Behind me, Gleeson scans the field from the turret. Nobody sees shit.

"Move to the tank," my Motorola says quietly in Kurtzson's voice. "Confirm that it's derelict."

I push the radio against the plate inside my vest, the reason it's so goddamn heavy, the part that stops things from passing through me, and press the soft rubber button. "Roger," I say.

The dismounts walk through the knee-high vegetation. I smell burning, but from a long way off. I hear cars in the distance. The tank looks asleep. There are small irrigation ditches every few meters, maybe a half-meter deep. Some have dark water in the bottom of them; most are just damp. I jump over them. I'm wearing a Kevlar helmet with a too-loose chin strap, knee pads that stretch from mid-shin to mid-thigh, a cod flap that hangs to my knees, and a vest that weighs seventy pounds, loose around the middle because the heat is melting me away at a rate of seven pounds a month. I feel like a child who tried on Mom's too-big dress, and heels, and wig, and then wore them off to war.

Mid-trench-jump, growing out from the dark earth through green blades of grass at my inevitable point of impact, the tail fin of something unexploded is sticking up and out, straight toward me.

My throat makes a noise that sounds like "Fuck!" but my mouth isn't open. I spread my feet hoping to straddle it, and it works, except the inertia of my seventy-pound dress and flap and pads continues pulling me forward until I fall directly over it, onto one hand and two knees, the other hand fighting to keep my rifle out of the dirt. Between my knees, the back half of the ordinance is inches away from the crotch of my pants, cod flap in the dirt, balls in abdomen. My mouth opens. "Fuck! Bomb! Maybe! Something!"

My grounded hand is sunk in wrist-deep. It's the only part of me not shaking. I suck in air, tighten up, strain to get my knees out of the soil. The blood pushes up behind my face, I see sparks. I push myself forward, onto my feet. The other dismounts come over.

When my sight clears I say, "Call the bomb guys."

"EOD," somebody else says and heads to the trucks to call.

The rest of us look at it. When I was about to land on it, it was the biggest explosive device I'd ever seen. Now it looks to be about ten inches long, only half of which is visible, dark brown and gray, and well-rusted. I walk back to my truck, brushing dirt off of my hand and knees. I have to shit, but fight it. I drink water.

Other dismounts make it to the tank. It is long-abandoned wreckage. There is no hope of finding the POO that brought us out here. And no more mortars fire. Our security posture incrementally relaxes during the hour we wait.

EOD pulls up behind my truck and two men get out. The small one leans against his door, looking us over. The tall one walks past me to where a few soldiers are standing around the ordinance. He's wearing a pistol rig on his thigh and bug-eye sunglasses. From four feet away, he looks at the tail fin and stops. "Who found it?"

"I did." I walk down onto the field.

"You called me away for this? I was balls-deep in a well-lotioned sock. For fuck's sake." He leans forward and pulls it out by its tail with his bare hand. I start to say something when he throws the ordinance at me. I don't even move. Its nose slams into the center of my chest plate. I swear something cracks, not my plate, maybe just my guts. It falls down between my feet. I open-mouth stare. I really think I might shit.

As EOD walks past me to his truck, he says, "It's inert, pussy. No boom boom." His mouth smiles. Behind his glasses I think he might have winked when he said it, but it doesn't matter. He's gone. I pick up the inert round and go to my truck.

"You okay?" Gleeson says.

"We sat here for an hour for nothing?" Napes says.

"Mount up," the radio says. We leave the green of the fields, everything turns brown again. I'm holding the ordinance in my hands. As it dries it lightens in color, but it's still a goddamn awful brown. The first two inches of it are bent at an odd angle, I think from its original impact in that field. I like that it's fucked up. I slide it into my cargo pocket. I scan. My hand already misses the feel of the blade of grass. Out my window everything slides by. My guts settle some and I tap my forward assist.

COWBOYS

The radio cracks: "Return to base."

"Thank fucking god," Napes says from behind the wheel.

"What's happening?" Gleeson asks from the turret, yelling down through his knees.

"Return to base," Hicks calls up from the TC seat.

"About fucking time," Gleeson says. "Sergeant Mills, can you pass up a water?" I hand him a bottle from the cooler which he built from an empty MRE box, a garbage bag, and now-melted ice.

We've been rolling for twelve hours. Patrolling the sector. It's eight o'clock and the sun's getting ready to set. The sky is reddening as the smog lights up. Our string of trucks speeds up, faster than we've driven all day.

"Slow down," Hicks says. "I want two more car-lengths between us and the truck in front of us."

"Just trying to keep up," Napes says. Hicks doesn't say anything and doesn't look to Napes. The truck slows.

Hicks asks, "You in a hurry?"

"No, Sergeant, just tired. Twelve-hour patrols are bullshit."

"What's happening?" Gleeson asks.

"This is bullshit," Napes calls up.

Gleeson shifts in the turret strap, bangs his heels against the platform like they've lost feeling. "What is?"

"Twelve-hour patrols."

"Oh, is it tough sitting down there in your padded seat all fucking day? If it ever becomes too much, you can sit your skinny ass in the turret, any time."

"Alright, that's enough you two," Hicks says.

"Chirp chirp," Gleeson says. "That's what your bitching sounds like. Chirp chirp, little Napes." He bangs his boots again. "Chirp chirp, Little Bird."

Buildings slide by. Smoke from garbage, piled up and burning, smears the landscape. Where a concrete wall lies collapsed, my view opens up to a parking lot. More kids than I can count are playing soccer. The ball goes wild and one boy goes after it—the rest leave it to him. They're smiling. This marks the end of our sector, our base just outside it.

On both sides of the road, walls run parallel to us the width of each house, all between two and three meters tall. Some are made of sloppily laid bricks. Some look like sand-colored stucco, with strips of green and white tile along their tops. A very few have streetlights mounted at their entries—deep yellow glass globes held in black metalwork. Beyond are the houses. Everything is rectangular—the brick and concrete of the ground floors, half hidden by their walls—the windows and terrace railings of the second and third floors. Small stacks of varying browns, sometimes pockmarked with the black of bullet holes or the too-light patching of them. Dark windows reflect orange in the evening sun. An endless, jagged series of right angles only sometimes given relief by nearly green palm fronds. It's the windows and terraces that I'm supposed to be watching but I let my eyes go slack, the houses and the wall segments melding into a solid, massive blur.

There's dead space between the road and these walls. The world already feels better—more open—than it does within the sector. One more turn before we reach the base.

Ka-ka-ka-ka!

"Contact! Contact! Shots fired, twelve o'clock!" Gleeson yells. He keeps his gun toward the right of the truck, but I can tell from his feet that he's looking out front.

The line of trucks makes the turn toward home, a cluster of police are at the corner. One is yelling into a walkie-talkie. One is holding his bleeding shoulder. Three more are screaming at each other.

"What the fuck?" Napes says.

The radio cracks: "Halt."

I see the towers of our base. "Goddamn it," I say. I just want sleep.

"Dismounts out," the radio says.

I scan the street from our truck out to about fifteen meters. There's some trash and gravel wind-caught against the curb but nothing bigger and no signs of previous digging. I scan higher, every window, every opening in the walls, every figure leaning out a terrace. Nothing threatening. Alongside our string of gun-trucks, all the dismounts are on this, the side away from the IPs. Maybe it's because the mounted machine guns are quietly taking their aim to the other side, toward the yelling. Maybe it's because our patrol is over and we're all done giving a shit today. But the security of it feels imbalanced. "Gleeson, I'm coming around."

"Cool."

As I circle the humvee, Kurtzson passes with the interpreter and two dismounts, walking toward the police checkpoint.

The sun is low now, orange at the shimmering horizon. I look toward the police, where the world is slipping into the inevitable red. Men gesture at Kurtzson, explaining. Gleeson is scanning over the barrel of his machine gun. He's a good gunner.

Inside the humvee Hicks is reading a Louis L'Amour. Napes is reading a *Muscle & Fitness*.

"Napes," I say, "put that fucking thing away."

"But Sergeant Hicks is reading."

Gleeson says, "Awww, Baby Bird. You're all fucked up."

Napes jams his magazine behind the radio mount.

Hicks says, "You know why I read Westerns?"

Napes, pouting, says, "Why?"

"I like to know how I stack up against the greats. Take Gleeson up there, he's twenty-eight or so, he's already outlived two-thirds of the Dalton Gang."

"I'm twenty-three," Gleeson says.

"*I'm* twenty-three," I say. "Whose wife did you fuck that you're still a specialist?"

"Just Top's, but I should have taken the rank."

As Kurtzson passes, I ask what happened. He says a black Mercedes drove by, fired out its windows at the police. Their own medics are on their way for the bullet wound.

"Napes, how old are you?" Hicks asks.

"Nineteen."

"Well, shit, you haven't outlived anyone really, but you're getting close to Billy the Kid. He died at twenty-one."

Tires squeal. A white pickup truck skids to a stop, doors open. Four men get out. One is bigger than the others, fat like a Westerner. The policemen start yelling.

"Me, I'm thirty-six next month, I'll be tied with Doc Holliday."

Two of the newly arrived men are collecting the policeman with the bloody shoulder. He screams. Fights. They drag him toward the truck and put him on his knees.

Custer died at thirty-six too, I think.

"I've already passed Jesse James, the poor bastard," Hicks says.

The fat man pulls a nickel-plated pistol from his belt, points it at the bloody man's nose. In the turret, Gleeson jumps out of his strap, rotates the barrel of his fifty-cal, stops at the white truck.

"Passed Bob Ford when you was still sucking tit."

My rifle is raised, but not high enough. It's pointed, but not aimed. There is no sound but the kneeling man is saying something, his mouth open and going. The other policemen are staggering backwards, stepping off the corner and into the street, trying to disappear.

"Sergeant Hicks?" I say, stepping toward the checkpoint, needing him to see this.

"Pat Garrett, fifty-seven."

My thumb rotates my safety selector to SEMI. *Click.*

The fourth man from the truck is at the fat man's shoulder, the pistol glinting red in front of him. The man on his knees sobs. The fat man looks bored. From fifty meters, I swear I see his finger tighten against the trigger.

I do the same, aiming now, at the fat man's cheekbone. Fuck center-mass.

"Bat Masterson, sixty-seven."

The fourth man, as lightly as a hand on a bible or a kiss on a child's forehead, sets his hand on top of the fat man's pistol, so lightly it doesn't move from the bleeding man's nose. He nods toward our truck, at Gleeson's long black barrel. I see his mouth move.

"Who the fuck is Bat Masterson?" Napes asks.

Like he couldn't care less, like he could take it or leave it, like it wasn't a man on his knees that his gun is pointed at, the fat man shrugs, and puts his pistol back in his belt. The bleeding man slumps in relief. The fat man turns and nods to the truck and the henchmen drag the policeman, throw him into the bed, and get in with him. The fourth man gets behind the wheel.

I lower my rifle.

"Geronimo was seventy-nine when he died."

The fat man, faster than fat people move, faster than I can tell what's happening, fires into the bed of the truck.

My rifle is up again. Behind me, above me, Gleeson wags his barrel from bed to driver to tires and back to driver. "Fuck," he says.

Tailgate down, I see the bleeding man, still alive, crying, holding his thigh, pushing against the blood that is coming out the color of the sky.

And they're gone. Rocks and dust dragging in their wake.

The radio cracks: "Mount up."

I'm back in my seat with my rifle set between my knees before I realize it's still on SEMI. *Click.* SAFE. But it doesn't feel like it.

As we start rolling, Napes says, "Why do you know all that about people's ages and shit?"

"I read."

"No, I mean, why their ages when they died?"

"Seems important, how long a person makes it." Hicks closes his book. "Once you're dead, the numbers matter."

Robinson,

You changed my name to Hicks...you must think the world of me.

Stone

BLEEDER

"How much?" I say. The man is smiling and blinking. He speaks but it's jibber-jabber.

"Sawyer, come on," Mills says. "We'll get something at chow." He's already walking toward the front stairs.

"Tea," I say. "Chai?"

"Ahh, yes, chai," the man says. He's shorter than me, with black, pushed-back hair and a Saddam mustache. Every part of him is thin except that mustache.

"You make me chai? Cold chai?"

"La, la, la, no more chai. Tomorrow."

"You make hot fucking tea all day long. Make me a batch. Put some ice in it—how fucking hard is that?"

"Sawyer," Mills says.

"No, I have American money and want some iced tea. It's not that complicated." Back at the FOB Mills is my roommate, always moping around, watching everybody. A real creeper. We're both buck sergeants but they gave me a truck and made him a dismount so, yeah. Fuck him.

My M-4 is laid across the restaurant host's small counter. I thought it would help him focus. The man is still blinking and smiling. "What is that, like a permanent expression? That your dictator affect? Jesus." I pick up my rifle.

"Shukran," the man says.

"Afwan, and fuck you." I follow Mills down the stairs and onto the street.

"Coming to chow?" he asks, nodding toward the hotel complex.

"No, I'll head to the Baghdad." I watch him walk into the serpentine, into the dark. I'm still thirsty.

Under the streetlight, prostitutes are starting to accumulate. I look for the one most American-looking—the one showing the most skin. They're all looking back but some are in dresses, some in head coverings. "You," I say. A girl in a cut-off t-shirt and too-small jean shorts clops her way over to me in honest-to-god heels. It could be any sidewalk anywhere. When she gets to me she puts a hand on my shoulder, fingers skim my neck.

"How much?" I say, one hand around her middle, one on the pistol grip of my M-4. She's soft in my hand and smells like shampoo. She giggles and leans her face in, hair brushing my ear. I have no idea what the fuck she's saying. I thumb her bottom rib, her half-shirt covering my hand, me touching skin. "Call me Sawyer."

"Sawyer," she says.

I pull her in by her bones and she giggles again. I press my barrel against her thigh, where it sticks out the bottom of her Daisy Dukes. I start to thumb my safety switch. "How much?"

She says something else in my ear. Jibber-jabber. She

pushes against my rifle and there is a massive pressure in my chest, my hands go cold. I want her to tell me how much and she's not making a lick of sense, but I don't rush her—I can't commit money to her until my cock starts working. It's just hanging. I have a hold of my first woman since we shipped and my dick has decided to go fucking AWOL.

"You buy?" An old lady whose face is mostly forehead is at my elbow, out of nowhere. Her arms are crossed. She's tiny but severe.

"Are you the pimp?" I say.

"You buy?"

I try one last time to muster an erection, squeeze the handful of heat in my hand, but it's useless. I shake my head. The pimp walks off and the girl takes a half-step away, hair pulling free of my ear, leg off rifle. She giggles again but it's less romantic than before. I let go of her slow, my fingers drag down her side, catch on her shorts, I thumb her pocket on the way. "Oh well," I say. I find a twenty in my pocket. "Whiskey?"

She smiles, pulls a stray hair out of my chin strap. I know it's black but under the streetlight it looks gold. She lets it go. "Whiskey," she says, and she's gone.

I'm standing on the sidewalk of the two-lane side street that is now the entrance to the hotel complex, which means it no longer handles ordinary traffic. It's a hundred meters of serpentine barriers and spirals of stretched wire, meant to slow incoming vehicles. Twenty meters to my right is the humvee and squad that guards the entry, beyond which sit the Sheraton and Palestine Hotels, where media and leadership stay.

I keep my back to the Tigris—in the dark it's all rivers,

it's the rivers back home, it's the Columbia and the Willamette, it's the Clackamas and the Deschutes. It's a river that if I walked neck-deep into, it would carry me to the gray Pacific and that would be perfect right now so I keep my back to it.

Seventy meters to my left sits the Baghdad Hotel, where I stay. There's less brass at the Baghdad, better food, a 70's-era lounge with shag carpet and mirrored walls, and a guy who sells pralines and cream ice cream cups. I only come out for guard duty and to talk to locals. So far it's the best part of this fucking deployment.

The road runs along the river, a shithole park takes up the space in between. The combat engineers move dirt around it during the day but right now it's quiet. City lights on the far side of the water. It's a good place to fire rockets at us from, on that other side, but there's nothing happening so I'm standing between a gaggle of hookers and a herd of kids who are inching their way closer to me.

"Go away," I say.

"Money," one says.

"Money? For what?"

"We fight."

I pull a dollar out of my pocket. The talkative kid grabs the boy next to him and they wrap arms around each other. Talker's knee buckles and they both go over, the kids around them cheer. They roll around on the pavement trying to pin the other's shoulders like they were really wrestling, but it's boring as shit so I say, "Time."

They get up and come over, both smiling. Talker was on top when I called time so I give the buck to him. They run back to the group and all the boys start yelling. It's all jibber-jabber and nobody's pairing off. "Somebody hit somebody else," I say.

Two kids grab each other and the others cheer. I look at my watch. Nothing much happens for thirty seconds and I call time. I give the kid on top a dollar. Both are smiling. I still feel the girl's hair against my ear. Smell the river in the wind. I want to do this for the rest of the deployment.

"Somebody hit somebody else." Two boys fall down and everybody laughs. I laugh, lean against the lamppost, and look at my watch.

"Jesus." Behind me, Mills is coming back from the serpentine barriers. He's such a goddamn sad-sack.

"What?" To the boys I say, "Time." They get up and I hand one a dollar. The rest of the group starts talking all at once.

"What are you doing?" Mills says.

"Nothing, I was bored. Somebody hit somebody else." Two boys hit each other and hit the ground.

"How long has this been going on?"

"For as long as man has existed." Mills doesn't laugh but I do. The kids are cheering. I look to the prostitutes, try to see the girl I gave twenty bucks to. They are at the mouth of an alleyway that fades into the unknowable. I want my goddamn whiskey. I look at my watch.

One kid catches an elbow and cries out. "Time!" I say. The boys stand up, one bleeding from his mouth. "This is why we can't have nice things." I hand the other kid the dollar and he runs off. The bleeding boy walks back to the others, pulling his shirt to his mouth, soaking up blood. As it spreads across the cloth my face flashes hot, hotter than the night air. The smell of the Tigris turns sour and the wind stalls. It comes up from the other side, a garbage gust of wind blows fresh from the alley instead.

"This is some bullshit," Mills says. To the boys, "Go away." They just look at him. "Fuck off, you don't need to fight." They look to me.

"Somebody hit somebody else." Two boys hit each other and hit the ground. I look at my watch. Fuck Mills. I scan the boys' faces and they aren't smiling. They're yelling and pawing each other and it's goddamn ruined.

From the alley behind the hookers, the kid who busted the bleeding kid's face is coming back with another, a huge boy almost the size of me, but fatter. There's pressure in my chest and I swear to god I feel my dick move. "Here we go. Somebody's ready to make some fucking money. Time!" The two fighters stand up. Neither has a mark on them but one is starting to cry. I hand a dollar to the other.

The big kid steps up. "I fight. I fight."

"Okay. Who?"

The fat kid turns to the group of boys. They all shrink back except the kid with the bloody lip—he steps forward, dropping the front of his shirt.

When they stand facing each other, it looks hilarious. David and Goliath, if they believed that sort of thing. Bleeder looking up. Fatty looking down, smiling.

"Don't fucking fight," Mills says. Nobody moves.

"Somebody hit somebody else."

"Don't—" Mills begins and Fatty grabs Bleeder around the neck in a sort of bear hug. Mills wants it stopped; he starts to raise his rifle at them because that's how we stop things. If they were Iraqi cars Fatty would be a black Mercedes, Mills would just shoot him in the hood as a warning shot. I laugh out loud at the thought of a round blowing through Fatty's grill and him slowly backing out of the fight, leaving little oil spots behind him. Mills lowers his rifle.

Fatty cranks Bleeder's neck. Bleeder winces. They fall, Fatty landing on top. Fatty hits like he knows how to hit. The other boys who cowered a few minutes ago when it was time to pick an opponent are cheering—rooting Fatty on.

From the bottom, Bleeder is fighting back. He's pounding small fists against Fatty's chest, doing no damage, but he's fighting back. Fatty lands a fist to Bleeder's mouth. His hand comes away bloody. My hand is cold around my pistol grip and my cock is at half-mast. I can't smell her shampoo but I'm almost sure I taste iron in the air.

Mills steps forward but I catch his arm. "Don't, they want to fight. Nobody's here by force."

He pulls his arm free. "They're here because you're giving away dollars and they live in a shit-hole."

I shrug and turn back to the fight. They've rolled onto their sides, slapping one-armed at each other. The other boys are standing over them, yelling nonsense. Fatty grabs Bleeder's hair, pulls, and slams his head into the street. I am rock hard. I smell shit and garbage and blood on the wind. My hands are still and cold and my chest loses its pressure all at once. Fatty lifts Bleeder's head again, brings it down without argument. The dull thud bounces off the buildings and cement barriers, across the broken park and down the banks of the Tigris.

"Time."

The boys are quiet. Fatty makes his way up. Bleeder is lying on the street. Fatty comes over to us, to me, his hand out, palm up. Bleeder starts checking his head for leaks. I hand Fatty a dollar. He looks down at the bill and back at me and says, "Money." He pushes his upturned palm at Mills and me, wagging it between us. "Money."

Letting his rifle hang freely from where it's clipped to his vest, pulling his hand behind him as far as it goes, Mills slaps Fatty in the side of his face. I jump at the sound, it happens so fast. Fatty falls on his ass, holding the dollar up the whole way down, like he's trying to protect something breakable. The handprint stretches from his cheekbone to his ear.

"What the fuck?" I say.

Mills stands over Fatty, who is rubbing the side of his face with his free hand, looking at me from under thick eyelids. The eyelids of gunmen with nickel-plated pistols. Of Iraqi police who used to be Republican Guard. Of men who've lived long enough and eaten well enough to be fat and old in this goddamn country. He gets up and walks slowly away, dollar in hand.

The other boys run away into the dark, leaving Bleeder sitting alone.

Mills takes a twenty out of his pocket and presses it into Bleeder's hand. He helps him up and Bleeder's off and running as soon as he's free of him. Mills just stands there, looking into the dark. He starts to wobble, takes a few steps to the edge of the street, and throws up everything he ate at dinner chow. He spits a few times, leaned out over his rifle. Wipes his mouth with his sleeve. The closest hookers walk over to him, put their hands on his bent-forward back. They talk quietly but it's all jibber-jabber. "No, thank you," he says. "I just spent the last of my cash." At the sound of *no* they leave him, and he heads off toward the Baghdad. I think he's too soft for this war.

"Sawyer." My girl from earlier steps out of the alley, paper bag in her hand. "Whiskey." When she comes close I breathe in her shampoo-smell and get a hand on her middle—on skin. I feel a quiet fire spark up in my chest. Through my uniform and her cut-off shorts, I press my cock against her. She presses back.

"How much?" I say.

STAFF SERGEANT HICKS GUARDS
A BOMB

The building was a remnant—the skeleton of an almost-skyscraper. Walls of brick and ragged cement. Glassless window frames. Sheets of plywood scattered across the floor, covering holes large enough to fall into but not through. Openings more than a meter across were left exposed. The biggest holes, large enough to slip a humvee into, began in the roof and descended through the next two floors, all caused by the impact of the same dropped and unexploded coffin-sized bomb. It was around that dull gray hulk, the shape of a shot bullet, that the platoon sat, four floors beneath the night sky.

The men wore clean, new uniforms. Their AK-47s were spotless. They were the masters of the remedial. There, on their mission to guard the ordinance until US troops arrived to inspect it, the clump of Iraqi guardsmen fucked off.

Small rugs were unrolled for tea steam and hookah smoke. There were three well-kept fires, ringed with brick.

In one corner, three men were piled up together, sleeping before their middle-of-the-night shift. A tore-open box of American MREs lay gutted nearby, the plastic packaging hissing and popping in the small fires.

At ground level, the building was surrounded by a ten-foot-high wall. Along its top, shards of broken glass, jagged green and orange and brown, ran along the straight line of masonry. At the front gate, under the yellow burning of a streetlight, sat three folding chairs, Iraqis in two, Staff Sergeant Hicks in the other.

Hicks was one of a handful of US soldiers charged with training the new Iraqi army, to live with them, to supervise their missions. It was supposed to be a rotation—a better assignment was coming. But the only rotation seemed to be between the old Iraqi army bunker he and the platoon lived in, and hard site security missions like this one. In between, Hicks trained his platoon, led patrols through the bordering neighborhoods, ate with his men, kept his door unlocked—once or twice even while he slept. His disdain for their greenness was eroded by their slow accumulation of casualties, until he felt something like admiration for those who hadn't deserted.

It's temporary, the battalion commander had said. *Back to a line-unit soon*, he'd said. In the cool air of the BC's office, stomach full of hot chow and coffee, morning sun glaring across the impossibly well-varnished desk, his company commander nodding next to him, Hicks had thought that *soon* was the wrong word. It had been three months since he'd caught those orders.

"Jesus I'm fucking tired," Hicks said.

The Iraqis looked at him but didn't speak. One pointed to the entrance of the building.

"No," Hicks said. "Not yet. I'll sleep when we get relieved." He took out a long strip of jerky. Began to gnaw. He waved the stick at the Iraqis. They shook their heads no.

Hicks's radio cracked: "Romeo to Golf, over."

Hicks pushed the button. "This is Golf, over."

"We have movement in the field to the west, break, possible dismounts, over."

"Roger, possible dismounts to the west, break, continue to observe, over."

"Roger, Romeo out."

Romeo's non-codename was Robinson and he was lying on his stomach on the roof of the blown-out building, scanning. He was already the bunker's ranking NCO when Hicks rotated in. He only left his room to shit, shower, and run missions. When Hicks would press him about it, Robinson would say, *I've always been here—I come with the bunker.*

"What he do?" an Iraqi said. It was a fair question; there was no need for an observation post on the roof. The building was abandoned. If it weren't for the bomb, nobody would be there. Hicks thought about why Robinson was upstairs.

"Security," he said. The Iraqis nodded.

The radio cracked: "Confirmed dismounts, break, maneuvering south around us, break, firing warning shot, over."

Bang.

Hicks looked to the roof, stood up, dropped his jerky.

"Negative, negative, cease-fire," he said into the radio. "Repeat, cease-fire."

Bang.

The Iraqis jumped up, grabbed their rifles from where they were leaning against the wall. They were talking fast, pointing to the roof. Hicks cleared the door of the building and started up the stairs.

Bang.

"Cease-fire!"

Bang.

Bang.

Bang.

When he came out onto the floor with the ordinance, all the Iraqis were awake, spread out around the perimeter of the floor, scanning through the hollowed-out windows. Hicks kept running.

His legs burned as he approached the fifth floor and his lungs were on fire. His chest couldn't expand inside his vest, he couldn't breathe deeply enough. He went light-headed. Hicks hadn't counted Robinson's shots but one rang out every few seconds. He hadn't heard any incoming fire—no AKs, no explosions, no nothing. Hicks hoped it was an RPG team out there, that once they fired he could send his platoon of dismounts after them. If it was a mortar team it would be worse. The two Americans would be pinned down on the roof when the bombardment started, their Iraqis still downstairs, not maneuvering, awaiting orders. Hicks thought, *Could a lucky mortar detonate that bomb?*

Overcoming the stairs to the roof, he nearly went through the bomb-hole. He came to a crouch as he came up on Robinson, who was still in the prone, tracking something in his sights.

"They're moving on us," Robinson said.

Hicks stepped closer, sprawled out on his belly, and

inched his rifle up to the building's edge. His elbow caught Robinson's flask, knocking it over. Bourbon-smell filled his nose. "The fuck?" He picked up the emptying piece of metal, examined it in the dark.

"Shit." Robinson sat up from behind his M-4. Clicked it to SAFE. Laid it down in the dust and spilled booze and Hicks's stare.

"Who the fuck are you shooting at?"

"Hajjis," Robinson said. "There's a group of at least five of them and they're maneuvering on us."

"You fired half a magazine. They haven't fired a shot. And this?" Hicks slapped the flask against Robinson's chest. "What the fuck is this?"

"Well it *was* Kentucky bourbon."

Hicks pushed himself up onto his knees, reached back nearly to his boots, and threw the flask over the side. It flashed silver as it ascended, spinning, a jagged piss-trail of liquor following behind. Momentum failed and the flask fell into the black shadow of the building. Robinson leaned way out, tried to track it but his eyes blinked thickly and he lost it. "Great," he said, "it must have gone over the fucking wall."

"Sergeant Robinson, you're firing on a target you haven't identified, on a target that hasn't fired at us, you're well out of the ROE, and you're goddamn drunk."

Robinson stood. Picked up his rifle. "Don't forget, Staff Sergeant, that I am also wearing two rockers to your one." He reached his trigger finger up to the rank insignia sewn onto the front of his Kevlar cover, *tap tap*. Reached out to Hicks's Kevlar, *tap*. Back to his own, *tap tap*. Then to Hicks, harder, *tap*. "Listen, can you hear the difference?" *Tap tap*. And then, *tap*. "Your grievances have been heard, and will be given my full attention just as soon as I give a shit." He picked up his rucksack and slung it over his shoulder. "Besides, who the fuck are you going to tell? And don't start counting Hajjis, not as people anyway." He started down the stairs.

Hicks stood looking at the blotch of spilled liquor. He looked to the field for signs of life. Nothing. Not even imagined ones. He started down the stairs.

When he reached the bomb, he told the men the shooting was done. They moved back to their fires and sleep piles. Hicks could hear the gurgling of the hookah resume as he continued down.

On the bottom floor, Robinson was lying on his back, head propped up on his Kevlar like a pillow. His M-4 across his chest. "Goodnight, Staff Sergeant," he said. Hicks went back to his chair at the front gate.

He found his fallen jerky, took a bite, and chewed. No RPG team, no mortar team, no enemy insurgents, no Mahdi Army, just people, walking through a field at night, and goddamn him for being drunk, for being here, with me, for being worse than the fucking mission, and how long does he have me, can he have me, running patrols with the Iraqis, while he sits on the radio, gets drunk, waits for the shit to start, and just listens to it, just listens, I can't, I can't, I need to get back, soon is too long, I've been hung out too long, I won't be hung out by him too, I won't, I fucking won't.

Knock knock knock.

It came from the outside of the rolling gate. The Iraqis pushed it open a few feet and stepped out. They came back in with two people. The man was thin, wore western clothes, jeans and a plaid collared shirt, and was clean-shaven and crying. The woman wore a blue hijab and was bleeding from her side. She was hugely pregnant. Her face was pale. She held a bloody hand out to Hicks.

Her husband began yelling. The guardsmen yelled back, gesturing for them to go back out into the night. Hicks ran to his gear and brought his medic bag to the woman. When he got close she laid that bloody hand on his shoulder. The husband pushed her hand off and shoved Hicks hard in the chest. He screamed and pointed at the wound and pointed at the roof and pointed at Hicks's rifle and screamed and screamed. The guardsmen stepped between Hicks and the husband, yelled back until the husband started pushing them too. Two rifles leveled at the husband. The woman bled silently, reaching her hand toward Hicks, a wisp of blood trailing from her finger.

"Stop!" Hicks said, forcing himself in front of the barrels. "La la la, no shoot, no shoot." The husband grabbed the back of Hicks's flack vest but didn't push or pull. Just held him. "Tell him," Hicks said to the soldiers, "I need to look at his wife's wound. I have bandages in my bag." The men spoke to the husband, not yelling but not quiet. They still gestured for them to leave. "Tell them I can help." The husband squeezed his grip on Hicks's vest, pulled him sideways, slamming him against the wall. Hicks fell onto his back. His medic bag crunched beneath him.

The rifles went back up, the woman's hand dropped. The husband screamed at the soldiers and braced himself.

BANGBANGBANG.

Hicks jumped at the sound, scrambled to get up but only made it as far as his knees. The soldiers looked to their AKs, then to each other, then to the husband, who was still standing in front of them, now quiet.

"Shut the fuck up!" Robinson said from the door of the building, his M-4 pointed at the sky. Everyone turned. Except the woman. Who just stood, bleeding.

Robinson came over, three stacks of American money in his hand.

Hicks stood. "They need to let me help her."

"That ship fucking sailed. Look at him, he's not letting anyone help her. I shot the bitch, I'll fix it." He held out the money to the husband. The husband spit at Robinson's boots. Slowly, without moving his money hand, Robinson raised his M-4 to the man's heart. He wagged the money in the air.

When the husband reached for it Robinson pulled it back. He extended his index finger from the same hand and pointed out the gate. "You take," he said, "and you fucking go." An Iraqi soldier spoke quietly over Robinson's shoulder. The husband nodded. Robinson lowered his rifle and handed over the bundled money.

"Take her to a hospital," Hicks said. To the soldier, "Tell him she has to see a doctor." The soldier spoke. The husband took his wife by the arm and led her out the gate. The soldiers rolled it closed. They went back to their chairs. Robinson went back into the building.

Hicks stared at his crushed medic bag. In the dim yellow of the streetlight, a dark green was growing on one side of the canvas sack, seeping black into the ground. His chest began to squeeze in again, half breaths catching in his throat. He dropped to his knees and reached two fingers to the darkening pavement, *tap*. His fingers came away muddy. He rubbed his thumb across his fingertips, felt the grit and grip of sand. Hicks unbuckled his medic bag. Inside, a punctured IV bag slowly bled saline into his supplies and into the dust of Baghdad. He stared at that for a long time.

At the end of their shift Robinson came out with their relief. "I forgot to tell you, this is your last night with us. You're getting rotated out."

"What?" Hicks said. "When did you get word?"

"I've known for a week. Said they're taking you back when they come for the bomb, you'll catch a ride with EOD. You're going back to your line-unit." To the Iraqis he said, "Open the gate. You two come with me. I'm adding a few more minutes to your shift."

"Where the fuck are you going?" Hicks said.

"We're going to go find my flask."

Robinson,

Why is Hicks the good guy? I didn't even
have a medic bag. I don't need to be the hero.
There is no hero in this story. And why the fuck
is the shooter called Robinson? You some sort of
martyr?

Fucking stop.

Stone

PEDESTRIANS

It's night, and we're driving around waiting for contact to find us. We listen for sounds of violence, we watch for flashes of something sinister on the blackened horizon. We are waiting. Always waiting.

"Think they'll hold chow for us?" Napes says. The dash glows softly green. In front of me he's just the negative space blotting out the glow, the shape of a Kevlar.

"Chow's every six hours," Hicks says. "We'll eat eventually." He's looking out into the darkness. The green light only strikes his shoulder and cheekbone. He's all structure and no substance in this space.

"I'm supposed to eat every two hours," Napes says. "How am I supposed to put on mass if the brass don't give a shit about feeding us."

"What's going on?" Gleeson calls down.

"Nothing at all," I say.

"I'm fucking hungry," Napes says.

"Chirp chirp, Little Bird," Gleeson says.

"That's enough you two," Hicks says. We are the last in line. Gleeson is facing the rear of the vehicle, looking out over our rolls of wire tied to the back hatch. His knees are next to my head. The wind coming in through the turret almost feels cool.

"Hey Napes," Gleeson says. Hicks clears his throat, continues to look straight ahead.

Without turning his Kevlar, Napes says, "What."

"How the fuck did you end up in the National Guard? I know they didn't let you eat every two hours at basic. How'd you survive, all malnourished and shit?" He's half yelling through his knees just to be heard. "How many dicks you eat to maintain all that lean muscle mass?"

"Goddamn it, Gleeson," Hicks says. His green hand rubs small circles into the black of his temples.

"Fuck you, Specialist," Napes says. "How'd *you* end up in the National Guard after being such an active duty super soldier?"

"Shit," Gleeson says, "I'm just here for the college money. And to get those spurs."

The radio cracks: "Report of small-arms fire across company net. We're going to check it out, over."

The other truck commanders, including Hicks, each in turn, say, "Roger." Message received.

"Sergeant Hicks?" Napes says. Hicks grunts. "What spurs is he talking about?"

"Oh, well in the Infantry, when you serve in combat you earn a Combat Infantry Badge. In the Cavalry, we earn our spurs."

"Actual spurs? Like jingle-jangle cowboy spurs?"

Hicks exhales hugely. "They don't jangle—one piece of solid metal. They're symbolic. Story goes that when green cavalrymen first made it to the front, they would hurt their horses something fierce if they were wearing spurs that first time. You make it through that first one, show your grit, your ability not to wreck your mount, *then* you get your spurs."

We turn. We turn again. We go straight for a while. I'm in the back seat of the trail vehicle, looking out the window, looking into nothingness, waiting for something stupid to happen. Or to not happen so I can go back to base and sleep. To set my rifle down against my bed frame, crawl into bed, and get through the fucking night.

Through the windshield, past Napes's hulking blackness and the other trucks, the headlights are reined in by a pedestrian bridge. When two trucks are past, two trucks still on this side, the air above the bridge lights up with AK fire.

Ka-ka-ka-ka.

The gunners ahead of us are orientated to the front and sides. All they manage is to hunker down into their turrets. We roll through, Gleeson stands up, off the turret strap, and our truck erupts with the sound of fifty-cal fire. Shells pour down from the big gun, clinking against the gunner's platform. Nobody says anything. Aside from the deafening shooting, it's so quiet I can't believe this is a firefight.

I turn around, unlatch an ammo can, and tear off the top—ready to hand it up when Gleeson runs dry. We're still moving as the long peal of shots begins to stutter and eventually breaks down into nothing. I hand the can up.

"What do you see?" Hicks says.

"A group of maybe five, taking turns at us," Gleeson says. He hands me down the empty; I throw it in back.

"Did they stop?" Hicks says.

"I stopped them."

The radio says something. Hicks says back that we are alive and well. We've slowed to a crawl.

"What the fuck?" Napes says. He's looking straight out his window. I pull the knob that drops my window. Barrel out, I look over my sights.

A car is rolling without power, past us in the oncoming lane. Its driver is dead—really dead. The windshield is spider-webbed and the man's head is tilted back. His jaw is slack, wide open, so open that *slack* is the wrong word. His eyes are sunken and his face is stretched; he looks like he's screaming but all I hear is the ringing left by the fifty-cal. His skin is gray, from the streetlights and from being fucking dead.

The moment my barrel flags him I feel like I just pissed on his grave. I pull my rifle in and bury it between my feet. We didn't kill him but goddamn if he isn't dead, while we roll by without a scratch.

Before we fully pass him, before Gleeson sees, I tap his knee. I wish someone would tap my knee. He looks down. "You alright?" I say, still looking out my window.

"Yeah. Fucking great," he says. We've passed. Only Napes and I have to know what the dead man looks like. Like he's screaming.

I want to go to bed. I want to sleep and wake up on a different day.

We pick up speed. Continue mission. Charlie mike.

"I'm so fucking hungry," Napes says.

Robinson,

    You think you are the only one who can tell a story?? I can tell my own fucking story, son. You can shove that Hicks up your ass, I'll write it myself. And it may not be as pretty, but it will be a damn sight more honest. You don't know shit.

Stone

THE HORSE LATITUDES

Combat patrol. Again. Our truck is last in line, Napes just follows the truck in front of us. Hicks is reading a book. The free election is coming up—we're making ourselves seen. This mission is to drive around for twelve straight hours—see what happens—and must have been thought up by a pogue who has never left the TOC.

Gleeson is up in the turret, facing behind us. Every once in a while he jumps to his feet and yells something in Arabic at a vehicle that gets too close, then sits back down on the three-inch wide canvas turret strap, and scans.

I'm in the rear left seat, looking out my window.

It's daytime. Brown blurs past.

"Hmmm," Hicks says. He turns a page.

The radio cracks: "We're going to make contact with the school up ahead. When we stop, dismounts out, establish security." The voice is Kurtzson's, coming out muddled through the speaker. We stop. Hicks turns a page.

On my side of the truck is a cement expanse, a slab of gray the size of a football field, edged by quiet streets. Garbage is blowing across it lightly—it could almost be leaves. At the far end, a group of kids are playing soccer. I get three soccer balls from the back of the truck, white with green Iraq-shaped blotches, Arabic writing. I drop kick them toward the game and the *thunk* of each kick echoes down the buildings. They don't make it, the balls land less than halfway across. To Gleeson, I say, "How's that side?"

"Can't see shit." There's a wall higher than Gleeson's chest bordering the school. "Just the schoolyard," he says, gripping the handles of his fifty-cal.

Napes drops his window hard, *bang*. Fear shoots up my neck, not because it was loud—because it was behind me. I give him a hard look through the windshield that he doesn't notice. Gleeson says, "Hey, Baby Bird, how about some fucking noise discipline?"

Up ahead, Kurtzson, an interpreter, and a few Joes walk into the school's entrance. We're only four hours into this fucking patrol. "Recess," Gleeson says, looking over the wall. Through the open window I hear Hicks say, "Hmmm," as he turns a page. I look away from the truck.

"Good book?" Napes says.

"It's interesting," Hicks says. I take a few steps toward the cement void, watching the soccer match.

"What is it?" Napes says.

"You ever hear of Selkirk? Alexander Selkirk?"

"Nope."

"How about Robinson Crusoe?"

"Sure, guy on an island, right?"

"Yeah, a guy on an island," Hicks says. "Well, Alexander Selkirk is the real guy."

Fifty meters beyond the soccer game brown houses stand with dark windows. It's noon. The sun has reduced my shadow to nothing.

"No shit," Napes says, "that guy was real? Wasn't he stranded for like, half his life?"

"In the novel it was a long time. Selkirk was only marooned for a few years."

A few years. *Only.* That's three times longer than this deployment.

"Huh," Napes says. "That's not so bad."

That's almost six times longer than we've been here so far.

"Well," Hicks says, "it was long enough that he started fucking goats." He's smiling to himself, I hear it in his voice.

"Fucking goats?" Napes says.

"Yep."

"Jesus."

"He did other things too, though. He read his Bible and domesticated cats to keep the rats from fucking with him. He was something else. Industrious."

"Fuck!" Gleeson says, ducking into his turret. A rock the size of my fist flies past our truck, past me, and skids across the pavement. Down the line of trucks I see a dozen rocks fly by, a few hitting truck-hoods. One gunner gets hit in the back. All gunners rotate their weapons toward the incoming rocks—into the schoolyard. Gleeson's arms are locked in line with his fifty-cal, a single, long, waiting machine.

"And he was lucky," Hicks says. "He was bound to be found sooner or later. He got picked up and took home. Others weren't so lucky. There's worse things than being marooned."

I move to the open window, look to Hicks. He isn't interested in rocks. I ask Gleeson what he sees.

"Fucking kids. They're all grouped up, with rocks in their hands." He ducks down again as rocks sail over. I step behind our truck, hear soft impacts behind me. And Hicks's incessant voice:

"You ever hear of the Horse Latitudes?"

"Nope," Napes says.

There's yelling up ahead. Two of the gunners turn their guns back to my side of the line, reestablishing security. Gleeson rotates his handles back toward the rear.

"See, Selkirk was well supplied, and was marooned with plenty to keep a man alive. But there are these two latitudes where the wind just dies, dead air, where a ship will just be floating, waiting for a breeze, going through their food, through their supplies, praying for wind."

Gleeson ducks. I duck. Two trucks ahead, the gunner, Specialist Mason, takes a rock to the side of his neck. He starts to rotate his fifty-cal back toward the school, but his TC, Sergeant Sawyer, is yelling from inside. He slams his turret stopped and jumps down into the truck. When he comes back up he climbs onto his roof, bags of candy in his hands.

"When the wind doesn't come," Hicks is saying, "men starve to death. It's time to eat what's in the hold—it's time to eat the horses. Hence, the Horse Latitudes."

Mason is throwing candy as hard as he can over the wall, handfuls of it. He isn't saying anything, not yelling, just throwing for all he's worth. One by one, drivers hand gunners bags of candy, candy meant to be handed peaceably to children in the streets of Baghdad to promote goodwill. Now it's pelting the kids who threw stones at us. Before the stones, though, there was the occupation. Before that, the invasion. There's always something before.

"Eating horses is nothing," Napes says. "Fucking goats inside of four years…that's some shit."

Hicks turns for the first time since he started talking, to look at Napes. Through his window I hear he's lost his smile. "Son, you're in the Cavalry, it is not nothing—horses are *not* for eating. What the fuck is wrong with you?"

Gleeson shifts in the turret, glances at the line of trucks ahead of us, bursts of hard candy sailing over the wall.

"Do you want candy?" I ask.

"No." He looks over the wall. We hear screaming and chaos beyond it, but it's excited screaming. As hatefully as it's being thrown, they *are* getting candy.

"Chalk-o-lot! Chalk-o-lot! Chalk-o-lot!"

"Alright, alright," Napes says, "I take it back. Don't eat horses. Fucking goats makes way more sense."

"Goddamn right," Hicks says.

Kurtzson and his entourage come out of the school quickly, but not running. "Mount up," he says over the radio.

Eight more hours of combat patrol. Hicks turns a page.

I watch Gleeson, sitting in his turret strap, only exposed from the dogtags up. Arms relaxed some, fists melting into his gun. The sleeves of his blouse flutter as we roll, but from where I sit, it feels like the wind has died.

STAFF SERGEANT HICKS TAKES A DRINK

Coming out of the elevator onto the sixth floor of the Baghdad Hotel, you have two choices: you walk out onto the roof, where our observation post is, or down a hallway of doors. There are three doors on one side, none on the other, and one at the end. I go into the room at the end, lean my rifle against the nightstand, and lie facedown on the bed. I breathe in the scent of the woman who made the bed this morning. Rose water? Detergent? Either way it gets me half hard just knowing my sheets passed through female hands.

Through the wall I hear glass explode against something structural—the tinkling of fragile shrapnel. "Sergeant Hicks?" I say, face still buried in scent.

Nothing.

I pick up my rifle, go out, and knock on the door.

Nothing.

Inside, dim light from one bulb. Hicks is sitting on the

bed in his pants and boots. He has no blouse and no undershirt. He's wearing his green, shitty, Army-issue suspenders. And dogtags.

"Sergeant Hicks?" He's facing me, swollen-faced and glossy-eyed, a bottle between his hands, elbows on his knees, looking down at the deceptive beauty of glass embedded in carpet.

"Sergeant Mills," he says, not seeing me. "Go away."

"Everything alright? I heard glass—"

"Everything's fine. Want a drink?"

"No." I look down the hall, step inside, and close the door. My boots crunch glass.

He drinks.

"Where'd you find the booze?"

"Confiscated," Hicks says. "Napes bought it off a Hajji on the corner. Outside the art gallery. I took it from him—we can't have the privates drinking." He holds it out to me, label up. Jack Daniels. I leave it there, hanging between us.

"Their supply is getting better," I say. "Last year they were bootlegging poison." This was in the briefings we received from the previous unit. They lost two men to shit-booze in this sector. Hicks drinks again. "Not worried about getting caught?"

With tight, small movements, he swings the bottle by its neck in a circle, until he sees a small tornado within. "Nobody comes here. Nobody from company, nobody from battalion. As long as the Joes answer their radio-checks, we're as good as gone out here."

I step in farther, past the glass, and sit in a chair perpendicular to his gaze. I'm looking at his bent profile—burned-down, waxy and drooping—his chest glistens with sweat in the light of the single lamp. His face shines too—he's been crying.

"Maybe you should put that away for the night," I say.

"Maybe you should shut the fuck up and get out."

"Maybe I should." He drinks hard, and looks me in the eye. His face glints yellow in the weak light. My eyes follow the tracks down his cheeks. He notices and looks away, toward the door. "It's almost midnight," I say.

His hands squeeze tight around the neck of the bottle, the friction of it squeaks, like a sob. His jaw muscles work like he's trying not to puke. "Tell me something Mills, your wife shave her snatch?" He wants this to sound hard, but he breaks on the last word and I see his lip shake from the effort.

I look at the near side of his face, like it's nothing. Like it's a piece of shit-brown scenery. Like I'm seeing it through the rear aperture of my rifle sight. "I'm on shift at midnight. Napes and Mason will be coming in."

"I bet she does. Bet she shaves it clean."

"They see you with that bottle," I say, "Kurtzson will give me your truck. They'll stick you in Headquarters, handing out shit-paper."

He drinks.

He's trying so hard not to shake, his lips turn pale squeezing around the bottle. "That's how they do it nowadays, shave that shit to nothing, like goddamn children. It's perverted. Your wife's a goddamn pervert."

"Sergeant Hicks."

"Me, I'm from a different time, I need a thick bush."

"Sergeant Hicks!" I stand.

He throws the bottle into the door, so hard he falls forward onto the carpet, onto the old glass, in time for the now-shattering glass to cascade over him along with the whiskey. He's drunk enough he doesn't make a sound when the shards push into his forearms.

I shake my boots, one at a time, so the glass comes loose of them.

As I leave I see where both bottles impacted against the door. From the floor I hear a slow whimper beginning. "I'm sorry . . . I'm sorry . . . ," Hicks is saying, as softly as bleeding. Not to me. Without looking at the wreckage behind me, over my shoulder I say, "I'm off shift at six. If you haven't bled to death by then, I'll come by and pull the fragments out. Don't let the men see this."

I pull the broken door closed behind me. My hand catches on the knob, won't let go, trembles against the cool metal.

In my room I put my hands in the sink, running hot water over them until the shaking stops. They are bright pink. I towel off and they go back to tan.

I put on my vest, secure my rifle, tuck my Kevlar under my arm, and go out. At Hicks's door I hesitate, lean in, listen. Nothing. I do the same at each door until I meet Specialist Burnside at the elevator landing, also dressed for guard duty. "Evening, Sergeant," he says. "Shall we do this?"

Burnside steps out onto the roof, into dark. I look back to Hicks's door. "Fuck," I say.

"Sergeant?"

"Sorry, nothing. I need a minute. To hit the latrine. Can you start watch without me? Tell them I ate some bad goat or something."

"Roger, no problem."

"It might be a while."

"I got you."

Inside Hicks's room nothing has changed except he's passed out. I prop my vest and Kevlar against the door. With my hands under his armpits, I pull him up to his knees and drag him onto the bed. I search his gear for supplies and find a medic bag and a rolled up undershirt. I take the Leatherman off the front of my vest and open the pliers.

I take a pair of rubber gloves and a disinfectant wipe from his bag, glove up, wipe down the ends of my pliers, pull the chair up to the bed and set the unlined steel trashcan next to it.

As I slip the undershirt beneath his near arm, he starts muttering. "Shouldn't have shot…shouldn't have shot her…" It takes some maneuvering to get at the inside of his forearm, him lying on his back. I bend his elbow into a right angle. Only sometimes does he fight me. With the nose of the pliers I pinch out a shard, tiny and shining in the yellow light. I drop it into the trashcan.

Tink.

Another slides out, easy.

Tink.

"She'll lose that baby…"

Tink.

"Sonofabitch…"

Tink.

I run a piece of gauze down the length of his arm. When it doesn't catch, I start the other arm. Leaned across him, arm bent up, the first shard I find is big and round. Hard to grip. It's from the bottom corner of the bottle. The pliers slip, snapping shut, pushing the shard in until nothing is poking out. He jerks his arm clear out of my hand, his face scowls, his teeth visible between his lips, gritted. I pinch the wound with my free hand until the skin puckers, and I fit the tip of the pliers inside. I squeeze, soft, until it resists. I pull. It comes.

Hicks's face is up and awake and looking at me. Our

noses, inches apart. Fighting for the same hot air with our shallow breaths. Bloody pliers caught between us.

"He shot her, Mills. Shot her from fifty meters, in the dark. 'She'll never find the front door,' he said. 'Go inside and we'll wait them out,' he said."

His voice is quiet—clear like he hadn't had a drop. His blinks are slow and wet.

"They came. They came. Knock knock knock. The front fucking door. Bleeding all over. Big as a house, she was. Him with her, all eyes and shadow."

I sit back. Drop the big piece into the trashcan.

Thunk.

Hicks drops his head and closes his eyes. I go to work on the smaller pieces. "I went for my medic bag. 'I got this,' he said, 'I shot the bitch.' Went to his rucksack, three big bundles. Handed them to the husband, real slow, one at a time. 'This one's for shooting her. This one's for the baby.' Waved the last bundle at both of them. 'This one's if she dies too.'" Hicks swallows loud. Tears trail down from his eyes to his ears. "Knock knock knock."

I place large rectangles of gauze along his arms and tape them down.

"He took it, he took that money. Shoved it right into his Hajji pockets. Took her bleeding and crying right back out the front door. I hate them. I hate them so fucking bad."

I drop the bloody shirt and gloves into the can. They don't make a sound.

"It hurts, Mills. It feels like burning."

"It will for a while, Sergeant. You need to sleep." I put my gear back on, turn off the lamp, and leave.

I take two steps toward the roof, but go to my room instead. I put my hands in the sink and run hot water. It's a long time before the shaking stops.

Robinson,

So, what? I'm the piece of shit because you caught me drinking one fucking night? Fuck you.

Stone

BAPTISM

The sun shone white against the chow hall trailer, lighting the day but bringing no heat. Sunday breakfast. Most of the battalion sat warm inside. At the round plastic picnic table out back, Mills, Mason, and Foster watched their breath between bites. "Security is way better than missions," Mason said, dragging a sausage link through syrup. "All the down time. All the phone center. Internet café. All the breakfast."

"Fuck that," said Foster. "Time *crawls* on FOB security. Give me mission rotation any day. It may not be fun work, but it fucking goes." He mashed his eggs with the tines of his fork until they were the consistency of hummus.

"I like the hotels," Mills said. "No brass. Sheets on the beds. It's almost like not being here." He began cracking up the shells of his hardboiled eggs.

Mason leaned in over his paper bowl of oatmeal, struggled

to dissolve a particularly difficult sugar clump, pressing with the round back of his spoon.

"You waited too long," Mills said. "It's too cold. Pour in a little hot coffee."

Mason dribbled his coffee and smiled at the resulting melt. "How was the week? I heard there was some shit."

"Who are you asking?" Foster said, scooping scrambled eggs onto toast.

"You," Mason said. "Mills is in my platoon, I know how his week went. Besides, he's an NCO—he's doing *just* fine."

"Here we go," Mills said.

"Only shares a room with one guy, doesn't have to pull TOC duty, doesn't have to clean the shitters—I can keep going."

"Of course you can. You can bitch all fucking day, except those shitters aren't going to clean themselves."

"Ha-ha," Mason said. "Eat a dick."

Foster took a big bite of breakfast. "Actually, something did happen." He swallowed. "I am now in the soul-saving business."

"How's that?" Mills said, pressing the whites of his eggs into salt.

"A couple of Joes in my platoon have been all worked up about this being the holy land and all. Said it's too badass to be here as Christians and not do anything about it. So get this…" Foster bit hugely into egg-slathered toast, "… they talk Sergeant Cortez into taking the Chaplain out to the Tigris and fucking baptizing them. I didn't even know. We roll out for what I thought was a goddamn combat patrol and as soon as we get to the river we pull over and out jumps the Chaplain and these two guys start stripping off all their gear and wading into the fucking water. And let me tell you, that water is no joke. The land may be holy but that river is *all* shit."

Mason sipped his coffee and swished it across his teeth. Mills bit through soft white, into firm yellow, salt striking tongue.

"And then," Foster said, "just as the Chaplain is dunking the second guy, the first one already soaked to the bone, guess what floats by, barely out of the mud?"

"No idea," Mills said.

"Dead goat," Mason said.

"Better," Foster said. "Dead fucking Hajji. Face up and everything, floated by close enough to touch, slow as anything, in no fucking hurry. But you should have seen the Chaplain scurry up the bank." Foster laughed hard, egg left his mouth. "And those sorry, saved, sad-sacks, trudging back to their gear, talking about probably needing shots." He drank orange juice deeply until the straw made sucking noises in the bottom of his carton.

"What did you do with it?" Mills said.

"With what?" Foster scraped his plate clean of egg remnants with his last piece of toasted crust.

"With the body," Mason said.

"What do you mean what did we do with it? We didn't fucking shoot it—we left it." He ate his last bite of breakfast. "We charlie-miked. Drove around for a few more hours, stopped at the hotels and had lunch, then came home. I'll tell you what, though, one of those hotels got themselves a George Foreman kind of grill and they're making melty sandwiches now. You gotta get over there and get one before they figure out we like them and stop making them. So goddamn good."

Mills sipped his coffee, watched the steam rise off and go. "You had a busier week than us." In his plate sat crushed shell, yolk, and salt.

Mason held his cup in both hands, thumbed its lip with increasing pressure, until it made a quiet *thunk, thunk, thunk*.

"The night before," Foster said, "we ran into some shit, some sort of celebration over a soccer win or something. Anyway, folks were drinking, enjoying themselves, and of course the shit-heads can't have that, so they started shooting up the crowd. Really brought down the mood." He pulled the straw out of his juice box, stabbed it into a chocolate milk. Began to suck. Swallowed. "We heard the shots from where we were patrolling, it was like two blocks away. We rolled up and fucking laid waste. The crowd had mostly left anyway, the shit-heads were just standing there blasting away with their AKs as everyone ran off screaming. And I'm up on the SAW, stoked to see my first fucking bad guy, you know? And I line it up and *Zip*—shit-head down. *Zip*—shit-head down. Felled them like they were made of balsa. We start taking fire but I'd already cut down half of them. *Zip. Zip.* I get now why that gun is called a fucking SAW. Inside of a minute we're just looking at an empty lot—nothing standing."

Foster's straw sucked air again. He piled his bowl, napkins, utensils, and empty drink cartons onto his plate. Took them to the trashcans. He stood looking into the black of the garbage bags. Mills and Mason finished their coffee and gathered up their plates and bowls.

"You shoot up shit all the time," Mills said. "What do you mean those were the first enemy you've seen?" He slung his rifle across his chest, squeezed the handgrip until the diamond pattern left an itching sensation in his palm.

"Well, I mean I shoot back when we take fire, but it's like they're invisible, I can never make them out. I just shoot at where I think the bullets are coming from. Or if something explodes, I just shoot across my entire sector of fire. But it's never an actual person looking back. This was the first time they were just standing there, you know? It's always so fucking spooky. It finally felt right."

As they walked toward the motor pool the sun shone yellow across the FOB, lighting the day but bringing no heat.

OBSERVATION POST

On the roof of a five-story shell of a building, all brick and rubble, overlooking the largest turn-around in the sector, is our hut made of boards and sandbags, just far enough back from the edge that it's only visible from the road. An eight-foot-high brick wall rimmed with shards of glass separates the complex from the sidewalk. There's a mosque across the street, a gleaming turquoise-colored dome surrounded by steps. Speakers for broadcasting the call to prayer.

In the hut are two green plastic lawn chairs; two pairs of binoculars; a shitty sketch of the landmarks in the turn-around left by a previous rotation; a wooden box with no lid half-full of fragmentation grenades; a handheld, unsecure radio; and us, Private Napes and me.

We're scanning our three areas of interest: the mosque, the turnaround, and the pita vendor.

Into the handheld, Napes says, "Roof to gate, over."

"This is gate, over."

"Roger, pita vendor approaching gate, break, send dismount, break, I want five-dollars worth, over."

"Roger, gate out."

To me Napes says, "It better still be warm." Everything is warm. At a minimum, if it's as hot as the air, it's 110 degrees. We resume our scanning.

Five minutes later Sergeant First Class Kurtzson comes up what passes for stairs in occupation-era Baghdad—all holes and treachery. He hands the plastic bag to Napes, who holds it up between us, showing off the condensation inside the bag.

"Wasn't expecting you, Sergeant," Napes says. "I figured you'd send up Burnside."

"I needed to stretch my legs. How's it look?"

"Good enough to eat."

"Not the pita, fucktard. The turnaround."

It looks brown. Except for the blue of the mosque and the blue of the sky, everything runs together, dust-colored. You have to look up for color, and I stopped looking up a while ago.

"No change," Napes says, pita already in his mouth, coming out at the corners, paste-like. I scan. Napes chews. Kurtzson waits. He's our platoon sergeant, he is supposed to check on each position, but he stands quietly behind us, unmoving, looking at the front of the mosque. He's tall, standing level with the roof of our little lookout. The sun is directly above him. I'm sitting in shadow, looking at him, he's all light. His face is angular and his gear fits like he's the prototype of soldier. His skin is tanned like animal hide from shaving with severity. He's just staring at the mosque.

Kurtzson says, "I ever tell you about the time in Storm—back when I was in the infantry, well, mechanized infantry—when we found that Iraqi platoon sleeping? Still in their bags?"

Napes says, "Nope," and pita spills out, lands on the toe of my boot.

"We just drove over them—*ka-thump*—they didn't fire a shot. Course, we didn't fire a shot either—they don't hand out CIBs for running them over." He scratches the spot on his vest where his Combat Infantry Badge is sewn to his blouse below. He's always scratching.

"No shit?" Napes says, chewing wetly—*smack smack smack*. Pita falls down his vest-front. It catches on the dust cover of his rifle.

I stare at the steps of the mosque, trying not to think about tires pushing bodies into sand.

"I ever tell you about the lieutenant that was with us on that mission? I was driving for him."

Napes shakes his head no. His helmet sits too far back on his head—like a child's cap. He takes another bite.

"Yeah, he was mighty worked up after I hit the first couple sleepers. Yelling for me to stop."

Smack, smack, smack.

I close my eyes inside my binoculars. I think about the drive out to the Blue Mountains in Eastern Oregon when I was a kid. How we swung up to Southern Washington to visit the lava beds first. How the road is a mess of smashed squirrels, hit by passing cars. How some get rolled from one end to the other by a tire and their insides blow straight out, leaving their hides mostly intact, but flattened. I think about sleeping bags.

"When we got back he tried to get me court-martialed,

but it didn't stick." Napes takes another bite. I was ten years old during Storm. I'm goddamn thirsty. "I got even with him though," he says.

He leaves it out there. He waits.

I was ten when we drove to the lava beds too. I open my eyes and scan.

Napes swallows. "Oh yeah?"

Kurtzson smiles so big I hear it behind me, the wet crinkling of lips stretching across gums and teeth. I can't look any harder into my binoculars. So hard I hope to come out the other side.

He says, "Yeah, once we got back to Germany, I paid this prostitute I knew to fuck him a few times, before he rotated stateside."

"That don't sound much like revenge," Napes says.

"No, it's cool. She had AIDS."

My eyes close, lashes brush lenses. I see bone and tissue push fast out the ends of squirrels and sleeping bags and uniforms, coming out the faces of Gleeson and Burnside and Mason, running over sand in every direction toward me and I'm in the middle of a black road, barefoot, my feet burning against the pavement and I'm ten years old, just standing, my feet burning and finally, the wet pieces of body and animal and blood get to me, run up over my feet and cool them, it brings me relief, and like a wave it passes, running down both sides of the road, a parting red sea, and where the road comes back I see Napes, lying on his back, wasted away, gaunt and translucent, where his lips are parted a kind of blue mold is growing out of his mouth and his chest is moving, up and down, up and down, up, then down, and it stays down, it just stays, and off the shoulder of the road is a ragged tree, Kurtzson hanging by his bent neck from a crooked branch, eyes closed, his mouth smiling.

"Well," he says, "you boys enjoy your pita." And he walks away.

Napes sets his bag of remaining pita on the filthy rooftop. I pull the binoculars away from my face and there are indentations from where I pressed myself into them. He picks up his pair and scans. "I guess we better not piss that guy off," Napes says. He wants to joke but his throat won't let him. It comes out wet and soft. Afraid.

As hard as I can, I throw my binoculars. From the roof, they carry over the gate, they fall slow and for a second I think they might reach the mosque. Instead they land in the nearest traffic lane. The tire of a bongo truck finds them, exploding the lenses out toward the sidewalk.

"What the fuck?" Napes says.

I clasp my shaking hands in my lap. "They weren't doing me any good. They're too narrow. There's too many to watch."

"Too many what?"

We sit quiet until my hands calm down. Napes doesn't eat anymore pita. Cars circle endlessly. Horns honk. Two kids pick up the scraps of rubber and plastic that used to be my binoculars. The neck strap is intact—one wears the broken mess like a necklace.

"How will you explain that?" Napes says.

"Field loss. Almost anything can be a field loss."

THREE STACKS

by SSG David Stone, retired

It was summer in Baghdad. They sent me to babysit the leftovers of the Iraqi army. There was nothing to do. Could not patrol because the Iraqis were too green. Tried cards, learning Arabic, reading. But XXXXX J____ figured it out. How to pass the time. He would XXX lie out on the roof, breathing in that cool night air that sits above the streets, sipping quietly from his flas

COUNSELOR

February in Baghdad is fantastic during the day. No sweat. No breathless evaporation. Just cool. I'm leaning my helmet against the window of the humvee. The seventy pounds of gear isn't so heavy sitting down but I can't get comfortable. Every couple minutes some part of me loses circulation—this shit isn't designed for napping.

Hicks is reading in the front passenger seat: *The Autobiography of Benjamin Franklin.* "He went vegetarian after he heard a trout scream," Hicks says. "What a pussy." Napes is racked out behind the steering wheel. We are staged, waiting to escort a group from Headquarters Company to Taji for a mail-run.

My door falls open, I almost go with it. I'm halfway through yelling what the fuck when Gleeson's face stops me. He has tears coming out of his eyes and he's breathing through his mouth.

"Gleeson?" I say.

"He's dead, he's fucking dead."

"Who's dead?"

"Hunter Thompson, he shot himself."

"Hunter *S.* Thompson?" I ask. He nods. "Jesus."

He just looks at me, waiting for something. I don't know for what.

"Mount up," Hicks says, startling Napes awake. I turn back to my open door. Gleeson is climbing up the hood, onto the roof. He drops through the turret with his full weight. The truck rocks so hard Hicks drops his book.

"What the fuck?" Napes says.

"Fuck you," Gleeson says. Hicks picks up his book and sets it behind the radio mount. Napes double-checks that his *Muscle & Fitness* is secure.

We start to roll.

Gleeson is facing backwards, his feet toward me. He looks down through his knees. "He was just sitting in his house. Nothing better to do. I think it was a forty-five, shot himself in the fucking head."

I picture a 1911 ejecting a smoking shell, watching the gun and the brass both falling, racing toward the floor, the gun being slowed down by the grip of the dead writer. I almost hear the *klink* when the shell lands first.

"He had his typewriter in front of him. The police found the paper still in it."

"Who shot himself?" Napes asks over his shoulder.

"Hunter Thompson," Gleeson says.

"What a cunt," Napes says.

"The fuck do you know, Baby Bird?"

"Suicide is a bitch move."

Gleeson stands up in the turret. We're moving thirty-five miles per hour. He turns his body, leaves the machine gun pointing toward the rear. He stomps on Napes's helmet. Hard.

Napes grunts and stomps on the brakes and I see Gleeson's feet leave the gunner's platform, he's taking flight. I dive after his legs, wrap an ankle up in my arms, pull him back in.

"You two knock it the fuck off!" Hicks says. He looks over to Napes. "I'll be goddamned if I'm going to lose a gunner to his own driver." Then up at Gleeson. "And no more kicking. The boy is already fucking addled."

Napes presses the gas, smoothly, and catches up to the vehicle in front of us. Gleeson regains control of his machine gun, squeezes its handles hard, thumbs the edges of his butterfly trigger. It's the shape of half a heart.

Hicks fingers the ragged corner of his book. Napes turns his head a few times, works his neck out.

"On the paper, the one they found in the typewriter, it only had the date and the word *counselor* on it."

I wonder if maybe he'd used a revolver. How much cleaner it would have been, not having loose brass falling. A wheel gun. Perhaps a Peacemaker.

"Writers are always killing themselves," Hicks says. "Hemingway used a shotgun, I think." He isn't speaking to Gleeson, he isn't trying to help, he's just talking into the space of the truck.

"Hemingway was a cunt too," Napes says.

"What do you think that means?" Gleeson says. "*Counselor…*"

I look up, to his face. He's looking out over his gun. I'm relieved he doesn't actually expect me to answer.

"It means he was a *real* cunt," Napes says. And Gleeson

is up and kicking again. First in the helmet and then on Napes's shoulder. Napes is punching back but there's only boots and kneepads to hit. Hicks is trying to wrap up the stomping feet.

Tires screech and I see across the truck and through the opposite window the blue of a bongo truck—the two-door cab of a minivan bolted to a flatbed; ten inches of metal railing wrapped all the way around. There are four men crammed in the cab and a dozen terrified faces, kids upon women upon men, looking back from the flatbed. Our humvee smashes into the side of the bongo truck. The driver brakes and it all slides out of view—all of them are yelling at us.

Gleeson stops kicking and stands up. "Fuck you!" he's screaming at the bongo truck. "Fuck you!" And his hands are squeezing the grips of his fifty-cal and his thumbs are flat against his trigger and every bit of him is shaking.

I'm just waiting to hear the shots.

"Gleeson!" I say.

The trigger pull is nothing, a synapse-fire away. The entire fifty-cal is rattling in its mount, radiating out from Gleeson's grief.

"Gleeson," I say. "Can you hear me?" I see his eyes try to look at me, but they fail him, they stay on the bongo truck that's drifted behind us. His wet eyes narrow, line up along his sights. "Gleeson, don't you fucking fire. I'm going to explain something to Private Napes. Don't shoot anybody until I'm finished. Okay?" He doesn't nod, but he doesn't shoot. Hicks just sits in his seat. Napes leans forward, away from me.

I slap the back of Napes's Kevlar so hard I hear his teeth snap shut. "Not one more fucking word. Unless you are reporting contact, not a peep." His jaws are working beneath his chin strap. "Maybe it's been so long since we shot somebody or rolled up on an IED blast site or since you experienced loss your goddamn self that you forgot what fallout looks like." Except for his jaw muscles, Napes doesn't move. "Just keep your mouth shut."

Hicks sits in his chair.

"Roger?" I say.

Napes nods.

I look up at Gleeson. I put my hand on his knee. "Don't shoot, *we* ran into *them*."

Gleeson sits down in the turret strap. He lets go of his fifty-cal, his arms hanging down, he shakes out his hands. There are still tears coming out of his eyes.

Hicks finds his book at his feet and thumbs it over and over. He picks up the handset for the platoon net. "All stop."

"Roger, all stop," the radio says.

"Specialist Gleeson," Hicks says, "you come on down. Sergeant Mills, you're up."

When Gleeson is in the back seat and I'm in the turret Hicks says into the radio, "Charlie Mike." Then to Gleeson, "You can't bring this shit outside the wire. Not on missions. I can't have it. You got to stow it, or…you just got to stow it." He opens his book.

As we roll I feel a hand on my knee. "*Counselor*," Gleeson says. I look down and he's stopped crying. "What do you think that means?"

THE COMBO

I t's my nineteenth birthday and I'm on fucking guard
duty. At the main gate, no less. Sergeant Mills must
hate me. Instead of sitting in a shack on the roof,
just me and Burnside, some goddamn alone time, Mills
puts me here. With him. And Burnside. So I know exactly what I'm not getting. It's like Mills knows too: Hey
Napes, I heard it's your birthday but I'm a total asshole
so let's hang out for six hours while I just sit here and
mope and watch you and Burnside stand ten feet apart the
whole night wishing you were upstairs or anywhere else
really and oh have I mentioned that I hate you?

Fucking prick.

But at least Burnside is standing ten feet away. He's
huge in his gear. All shadow under the streetlight but I
see his eyes, the brown of them. He's goddamn beautiful.

"Napes," Mills says.

I've been staring. I rub my eyes with the hand that's

not on my rifle. Maybe he'll think I'm just zoning out. "Sergeant?"

"Who's walking up?"

I go out past the last barrier, where the serpentine starts. The prostitutes are coming. A bunch of them. At least they're a distraction, something to speed up time. "Hookers," I say. Mills just sits against his piece of barrier.

Burnside comes out, looks the women up and down, then looks at me. He's close, his sleeve brushes my sleeve. Too quiet for Mills to hear, he says, "Happy birthday, you. I wish we were somewhere else."

"Anywhere else," I say.

He nods and I feel melting down my neck and back like ice water leaving my body. What's left is dry heat held in by my vest. I push my sleeve into his, my muscle against him. He smiles and steps away. In his arm's absence I stifle a shiver, squeeze my M-4 to my chest.

The prostitutes inch closer and closer until they are standing with us. A few Joes coming from chow at the Baghdad Hotel, heading to the Sheraton or the Palestine, stop when they smell perfume and shampoo and cigarette smoke exhaled by women. The more soldiers gather, the farther away Burnside stands. It's my fucking birthday and by achingly small bits, it's getting shittier and shittier.

I'm not the first to start in on them, these women who if pressed will attempt to repeat any filthy phrase, to get actual dollar amounts out of them. Blowjob, someone says. Two girls, says another. Four, says another. How much? Say cock. Say cunt. These men are fucking soft. The girls are all saying yes. The boys are standing with their dicks in their hands, money stuck in their wallets. I'm not buying either but goddamn, I feel like pressing, past where everyone else stops, I want things to be awful, to be ridiculous, to be a different kind of awful than this wanting, so I keep fucking going. I'm the last one in the ring.

"Listen," I say, "I'm not paying for one. I'll pay for two—for the mother-daughter combo. But that's it." I'm talking to the head woman in charge, Skeletor. Her face is soft brown, softer in this yellow light. "Take it or leave it." I see something spark behind her eyes and she heads to the edge of the light to talk with her stable.

"What are you doing?" Burnside says.

"Passing the time."

"And what happens if she says yes?"

"Look at them. They're all my age, there's no way she'll find a combo." His eyes are brown and close and I said look so he turns and looks and I can't see the brown of his eyes and I can't feel the heat under my vest anymore.

The men are all smiling at me like they're rooting me on, like what I'm pressing for is exactly what this birthday boy needs. But I'm not soft like them. I'm made better, stronger. I can push this. I don't want any part of it but goddamn if I'm not hard enough to go on.

Except for Burnside's eyes. They track Skeletor as she walks back into the light. "You are in luck," she says. "I have just what you want. Pretty girl, pretty lady, you like, you like."

Of course she fucking does. Why did I think there were limits to how terrible this could get? A woman comes out of the dark wearing a blue dress, her hair covered. She stares at the cement as she walks. Burnside's eyes widen as she approaches and a slow nod begins in his helmet: no.

The woman in blue stops at Skeletor's arm and looks from soldier to soldier, up to Burnside, down to Mills, over to me. Her eyes are black and crying.

"This is Napes," Skeletor says, "he very handsome man."

The cold at the base of my neck runs down the backs of my arms and settles in my palms. Where my hands are holding my rifle, I can't feel my pistol grip, my hand guard. The skin around my mouth squeezes tight and my eyes pinch and I'm looking at teary eyes and I'm smiling as hard as I can for fear that I'll start crying too.

Without looking away, the woman in blue says something in Arabic. Skeletor says something back. It sounds sharp. The woman in blue speaks. Skeletor screams. She screams and screams and pushes the woman in blue back into the dark before she comes over to me. From down the alley I make out sobs. "I make mistake," Skeletor says, "not this one. Her daughter gone, taken today."

"Gone where?"

"Just gone, taken, wherever women go when they go. It's okay, I have idea." When I look to Burnside I can't find his eyes. I turn away from the group, keep turned away until I think it looks like I'm scanning the serpentine. I can't breathe in big enough. When I turn back there is a tiny girl in front of me and Skeletor has a hand on her shoulder. They both step closer. The girl is young, shiny, like she's made of wet clay. She's wearing heavy eye makeup but it's ragged around the edges like she's just learned it. Burnside's helmet is still slowly turning back and forth: no.

"This is my daughter," Skeletor says.

The girl smiles. Skeletor smiles. I can't feel the rifle in my hands. I don't speak. We look at each other, on and on. Skeletor's mouth is moving but I'm sitting on the roof of the Baghdad Hotel in a guard shack and my knee is pressed against Burnside's and our rifles are laid up on the sandbags and we're taking turns looking out over the city and I'm calling in the sit-reps and he's telling me about how we'll move to Portland when this is over and our enlistments are up and we won't have to be hard anymore and we'll be soft but soft together which is way stronger than the kind of hard we have to be now and even in the dark we hear each other smile and the first few minutes after each sit-rep he'll hold my hand and in his hand my hand isn't cold and that's when I feel the tear fall clear to my chin.

"Napes," Mills says.

The girl and Skeletor are right in front of me and they aren't smiling. Skeletor's mouth is closed. I turn to the serpentine and wipe my face on my sleeve.

"Napes," Mills says. "Do me a favor and go to the Baghdad, bring me back a couple of those melty sandwiches. I haven't had chow yet." When I turn to him, he's getting up from his seat. "Can you handle that?"

Burnside is looking at me, his mouth a little open.

"Yes, Sergeant," I say.

"And take Burnside with you. In case they only let you sign for one sandwich. Don't come back without two, I'm fucking hungry."

Burnside and I move down the serpentine toward the hotel, him keeping his distance as we walk into the dark. The men start back in on the soft talk. I hear their laughing and the girls cooing responses until it's only our footfalls thudding in my ears.

"What the fuck was that?" Burnside says. He sounds more scared than angry and he slowly inches closer as we go.

"I don't know, I was just fucking around and everything fell apart. I don't know what the fuck I'm doing."

He keeps coming until our sleeves touch. "Are you okay?"

I push into him and my hands quiet. My rifle becomes solid again and its weight returns. "I'm okay. I was just fucking around. I want to be anywhere else right now."

In the hotel we order the sandwiches and go upstairs to wait. I drop my gear and lock the door and slide furniture in front of it. We spend ten minutes lying down, Burnside tracing the still-shiny tracks my tears took, our legs wrapped up together. I want him to talk about after, about the big what-next, but he's quiet and brown-eyed and goddamn beautiful so we just lie quiet. When it's time, I wash my face and put my gear back on. We slide away the furniture and I touch the lock but before I turn it he takes my chin lightly in his hand, leans in, and with eyes closed, we kiss.

OPSEC

We are third platoon. We are sitting in the room where the junior enlisted live. Sergeant First Class Kurtzson, our platoon sergeant, has called a meeting. It's late afternoon but it's dark inside, windows and florescent bulbs blocked out by hanging ponchos and poncho liners, still that decades-old Woodland cammo. The room glows green around us. "Platoon," Kurtzson says, "This is Private First Class Alvarez." We mumble something like a welcome. Alvarez is a backfill—ordered to a deployment that is already underway, to bolster a unit's roster. In this case, our platoon. It is an inopportune time to join a deployment. Being dropped in so late, it's likely that his presence will be resented. That we will resist. Therefore, he will receive minimal narrative attention.

"Sergeant Sawyer," Kurtzson says, "he'll be your new dismount."

"Fucking great," Sawyer says.

"Platoon, show him the FOB. Explain the mission rotations. Have him back after dinner chow—First Sergeant has a detail in mind."

"Roger," says Sawyer.

"Roger," we say.

Kurtzson leaves. Sawyer leads Alvarez out into the motor pool. We follow.

The motor pool is the dirt lot we park our vehicles in—a rectangle twenty meters wide, forty meters long, extending out from the exterior wall of the barracks building. "This is the company motor pool," Sawyer says to Alvarez. A wall of Hesco barriers makes up the perimeter of the motor pool. Hescos are collapsible frames made of steel mesh that support liners filled with sand and rock and whatever else we find nearby to make an instant wall. Zero actual construction and they stop bullets. Stacked two high, the wall is nearly three meters tall. Three orderly sets of humvees are parked along the wall, organized by platoon, with two more rows parked in the center of the lot.

Sawyer says, "Hesco barriers are—"

"He doesn't need to know all that," we say. "Just show him his fucking truck."

"That line of humvees is our platoon's," Sawyer says. "That one's mine—that's where you'll ride during missions."

We lead Alvarez from the motor pool into the open middle of the FOB. A paved road runs from the main gate straight across the small base and dead-ends at the base of the perimeter wall. On one side of the road sits our company's barracks, the chow hall, the helo-pad, the clearing barrels, and the gym. On the other side of the road are the buildings the other companies stay in, the battalion TOC, the medic's station, and the chapel. Sawyer points to two small trailers sitting next to our barracks, half hidden behind additional Hescos. "That's the shitter trailer," Sawyer says, "and that's the shower trailer. Don't fucking confuse them." Starting to turn in a slow circle, pointing at each tower on his way around, he says, "Those are our guard towers. One shit-bag in each, every minute of every day. If you're up there during chow time, the SOG will bring you a plate. S-O-G, that's Sergeant of the guard. Usually Sergeant Kurtzson or Sergeant Hicks. They run the shifts."

"He can figure all that out later," we say.

"When we take incoming—doesn't matter if it's small arms, rockets, mortars—when we start taking fire, QRF puts an extra Joe in each tower." Sawyer starts to walk Alvarez toward the main gate. "Q-R-F," he says. "Quick reactionary force. They respond to stupid shit first. And we all rotate through it."

"Stop over-explaining," we say. "He's full-grown, he can learn most of this shit as he goes."

Sawyer points to the front gate. "That's the front gate. When you're stationed there, you'll either be in that tower, waving the two-forty-bravo at incoming vehicles, or gate bitch—"

"Don't say it," we say.

"You'll open and close the gate," Sawyer says.

"Goddamn it."

"Next to the gate is our guard shack," says Sawyer. "We take turns sitting inside, in the shade, and we use it to store weapons we check from any locals who visit the FOB." He looks at us. Smiles.

We say, "Don't you—"

"FOB," Sawyer says. "Forward operating base."

"Cunt."

Turning to the middle cluster of buildings, "That trailer is the chow hall. That's the phone center. That's the Internet trailer. In that fenced-in section, that's where KBR lives." Sawyer smiles bigger. "K-B-R, that's Kellogg, Brown, and—"

"I'll kill you in your fucking sleep."

"—Root. You know, Halliburton." We just shake our heads. He walks Alvarez toward the chow hall. "Over there's the laundry. It's pay-by-item to have it done well or pay-by-the-bag to have them shit in it, run it through a dryer, and give it back unfolded." He looks at us, then at Alvarez. Back at us.

"It's true," we say.

"That's the battalion TOC," Sawyer says. "Tactical operations center. The brass run our little corner of the war from in there. They took most of our lieutenants, including our XO—yes, we had an XO when this shit started—which is possibly why we need backfills in the first fucking place. Anyway, avoid it. We have a company TOC in the barracks building, which you will sometimes sit at and be bored."

"The big warehouse-looking building is the FOB gym," Sawyer says. "On the far end are the barber and the Hajji shop. The barber does a good job but will undoubtedly rub his cock against you the entire time his shears are running. Which you might not be into yet, but you just fucking got here. Eventually, well, even Top gets his high-and-tights there." Sawyer's fade is immaculate. "And go easy in the Hajji shop," he says. "The DVDs are mostly bootlegs and only about two-thirds actually play."

"Why are you telling him about non-mission shit? None

of this fucking matters. Keep this up and you can establish the setting by your goddamn self."

"And the owner is all fucked up," Sawyer says. "Makes all this American money, runs low on stock, buys up more shit off the local economy, *pays* with American money—obviously working with the Army. So they kidnap his kid, ask for some of that good American money as ransom. He pays, gets his kid back, and then does it all again the next time he has to stock his shop."

"Why does he need to know that? Fucking Christ."

Sawyer does one more slow rotation, eying the perimeter wall until he comes back around to Alvarez. "Okay, that's all you need to know about the FOB. The rotation works this way—we have three assignments: FOB Security, which we're on now, towers and front gate; Missions, which is when we leave the FOB to do stupid shit like patrol and mail runs and hard site security; and the Hotels, where we babysit the complex where media and brass and whothefuckknows hang out. Each rotation lasts a few weeks. Missions are the shittiest, obviously. QRF is part of that. The hotels are shitty too, but we get away from leadership, so it's less shitty. And security is the least shitty. Other than when your ass is in a tower, it's just down time. Except when Top comes up with a detail. We should hit up chow so we can get back. Oh, and Top is what we call the First Sergeant."

God knows how long he'll take in the chow hall, and we're all done with this expository bullshit. "No chow for us," we say. "We only eat with soldiers, and until Alvarez takes some fire, a soldier he fucking ain't." Sawyer walks Alvarez into the chow hall. We go off toward the barracks. And wait.

After dinner, Sawyer takes Alvarez to Kurtzson's room. We watch. "Go to the bookshelves in the dayroom," Kurtzson says, pushing two stacked cardboard boxes, cubes measuring a half-meter in each direction, into Alvarez's arms. "Fill the boxes with books. Take them out back to meet up with Top."

"Roger," Sawyer says.

"Not you, Sergeant," Kurtzson says. "Let the Private do it." The top box falls out of Alvarez's arms.

"He looks like he could use a hand," Sawyer says. They go out.

Down the hall they find two floor-to-ceiling book-shelves and begin clearing them. "Donated," Sawyer says. "One cool thing about the Guard is that when we all ship from the same place, all of us from Oregon, they do a pretty good job sending you shit. Care packages. Holiday stuff. Sometimes it's work, like an entire elementary classroom sending you letters, kids asking how it feels to kill people and get shot at and shit. Sometimes it sucks. But then, like this, the wives get a bookstore to put out a donation jar and within a couple months, have enough to send us a library worth of books. New books."

Sawyer and Alvarez carry their piled-up boxes out back, to where Top is standing beside the burn pit. We stand around, watching. The smoke comes up black like a garbage fire. "Dump them here," Top says, indicating the stack of books already at his feet, a few more in his hands. Sawyer looks to us but we don't look him in the face. He dumps his box. Alvarez dumps his. "What are you waiting for?" Top says. "Go get another load." He tosses a book onto the fire.

"But—" Sawyer begins.

"But what, Sergeant? Didn't your platoon sergeant tell you that the FOB is going back to the Hajjis when we leave?" Top drops another book, the smoke turning gray. The fire spits. "These are good American books. I'll be goddamned if we're going to leave them to be read by locals. *Don't leave nothing for the dinks.*" We laugh. Another book goes into the fire.

"The dinks, First Sergeant?"

"Christ on a fucking cross, Sawyer, have you never seen *Platoon*?"

"I've seen *Platoon*, First Sergeant. But I don't remember there being a book-burning in it."

Top steps close to Sawyer, has to look up slightly to stare him down. "This is no goddamn book-burning, Sawyer. It's fucking OPSEC. We destroy anything they can use. If we go to the trouble to burn envelopes with home addresses on them, why the fuck would we let them have a whole library of books. Use your fucking head."

To Alvarez, Sawyer says, "OP-SEC. That's Operational Security. And this is fucking bullshit." He's putting himself on the outside, distancing himself from us. For this, there are consequences. So we smile as we watch.

"Get the fuck outta my sight," Top says. "Report to the CO. I say carry books. You say it's bullshit. Sounds like an Article 15 to me. Alvarez, go get another load. Keep getting loads until that library is empty. I don't want to see so much as a jerk-mag on those shelves."

Sawyer says to Alvarez, "Article 15. That's a nonjudicial punishment, most often imposed by a commanding officer." To Top, he says, "And there's no fucking way the CO will."

"We'll see. Now move."

Alvarez follows Sawyer back into the barracks. Top picks up an armful of books. "Spell it with me, boys," he says. We gather around.

"A." He drops a book onto the fire.

"R." He drops another.

"T." Another.

"I." We chuckle.

"C."

"L." We pick up books from the pile.

"E." Top drops a book.

"Fif…" We drop a book.

"…teen." And another.

We are throwing in books and the fire is spitting and cracking, the heat pushes back at us but we're used to the heat—we have acclimated. The smoke is coming up white and we are laughing. Alvarez is bringing the books.

Robinson,

All right, I'm not writing any stories down. There's no point. But you shouldn't either. Not if you're only going to write me as a drunk mess. You're missing the goddamn point, Matty. I have to live with it, that blood and money and gut-shot Hajji. I'll never XXXXX. You can't even write it? Do better.

Stone

COFFEE & BAKLAVA

It's afternoon and somewhere around 105 degrees. But that's air-temperature. It's not taken from between my scalp and my Kevlar, or down in my boots, or in the space between my vest and lower back. In these places it feels like water's boiling just standing around. So we hide in the shade.

The last humvee in line rolls past. Its gunner pulls back his charging handle, pushes it forward. Napes walks through the diesel fumes, pushing the front gate shut. It's nearly three meters tall and more than four wide—a big squeaky bastard, sheet-metal welded over steel beams, all of it painted the color of afternoon sky, but flaking, so rusty-orange comes through in places. He comes back to our shack and sinks into his nylon camping chair. "Mason, you get the next one."

Mason is reading Gleeson's disintegrating copy of *The Rum Diary*. "Shut the fuck up." Continues reading.

Against the perimeter wall, overlooking the main gate, and the serpentine beyond, Gleeson sits behind the two-forty-bravo of the guard tower. "One pedestrian coming up. Looks like an IP."

Pushing the gate open a foot, I let in an Iraqi policeman carrying a small plastic bag with a white pastry box inside. He hands it to me, I hand him a twenty, American. We shake hands and he walks away.

"What's that?" Napes asks.

"Baklava."

"What, you're going to eat it?"

"What the fuck do *you* do with baklava?"

Sitting in the shack I take the box out of the bag and set it lightly on my knees. To buy something not from the Army feels like a privilege. I pry the lid back, lean over the box, and inhale deep.

Honey. Pistachio. Dates. I swear to god, after this breath I know what *flaky* smells like.

Napes is hovering. "You're really going to eat it? It's Hajji food. Could be poisoned."

"Fuck you," I say. "Gleeson," I call up to the tower. "Can you see which IP brought me my box?"

Gleeson looks over the wall and down a ways to the gaggle of men standing in the shade of a pop-up awning. "Yeah, I see him."

"If I die after eating my baklava, shoot him."

"Roger."

The filling is gooey in the heat, my fingers absorbing the sweetness, becoming sticky. I put the whole piece in my mouth, my jaw straining against my chin strap. I close my eyes. And chew.

I feel Napes watch me. Hear his mouth salivate. He

licks his lips. Mason leans forward, sniffing at my happiness. And then they both disappear. There's nothing but my mouth and this baklava and goddamn elation. Nutty sweet crunchy soft perfection. I chew longer than I need to, but I'm not ready to stop tasting it. I'm outside the FOB. I'm walking through the date field barefoot, surrounded by green, the feel of grass between my fingers. I'm in the Blackhawk taking us to Taji, second stop before home, face full of wind and moonlight. I'm signing my rifle over in Kuwait and I don't reach for it out of habit, not once, I'm almost home. I'm sitting at a table in Portland, my hand on hers, I'm eating baklava and she's laughing.

I swallow, open my eyes, blink them clear.

"Trucks heading out," Mason says.

Napes opens the gate and I hear trucks pass behind me. As I step out onto the roadway the last truck rolls past. Its rear tires hit the tracks of the gate and bounce the gunner hard.

Bang!

The fifty-cal round passes between Napes's head and my face, taking with it most of my air. It impacts against the perimeter wall on the other side of the FOB, just missing the legs of a guard tower.

Everyone's up: Gleeson shouldering his machine gun in the tower, Mason out of his chair, his book underfoot, Napes still by the gate but half behind it, fixing his eyes on the gunner. In my throat, baklava is creeping up. "Nice shot you fucking retard!" Gleeson yells, but they're gone.

Napes rolls the gate closed. Mason picks up his book, knocks the dust off it.

"You alright?" Gleeson says.

I swallow again and again, I can't breathe and the baklava

won't go down. My stomach is squeezing and my hands are scrambling at my throat. Choking. I start to retch. Mason slaps my back too hard and I puke, volley after volley, food catching on the backs of my teeth. I spit. Honey and sour across my tongue. Mason hands me a water bottle and I suck until it's empty. I am gasping.

Gleeson calls down again, "Mills, you alright?"

I can breathe, I swallow a couple more times. Wipe my mouth on my sleeve. "Yeah. I'm good. Just a dumb fucking accident. Gunners don't go red until they're out the gate. Till they're over the hump and rolling. He just charged it too soon."

We stand, looking at the gate, at its flaking paint, in the direction of the shooter. I look the other way, after the long-gone round.

"I got the bumper number," Mason says. "We'll report it to the SOG. That gunner owes you an apology. I know it wouldn't matter much. It's the principle." He sits back down. "I mean, no apology's going to undo a fifty-cal round."

In the shack I pick up my box and sit, looking down at my baklava. My mouth tastes like puke. I pull out a piece, bite, and chew.

Thirty meters farther in from the main gate is a shed slightly larger than our guard shack, three-ish meters square, where the interpreters wait to be of use. Like everything else, it's brown. There's a door and no windows. It's late afternoon and there's a breeze, so the interpreters are all sitting outside the door. They're gathered around something silver—they're talking but I don't understand. Today all the interpreters are women. The wind gusts and

I breathe them in, perfume and soap and bodies. "Napes," I say, "go see what they're doing." I nod my helmet in their direction.

Napes gets up slowly, loaded down by gear, and begins walking. As he approaches, everyone stands and steps away from the door except one, who carries the silvery something into the shed. Napes begins talking, but very quickly he is drowned out. The interpreters are gesturing but it's lost on us. Napes backs away.

"Alright, alright," he says. "Fucking Hajjis." He returns to his chair.

"Well?" I say.

"They're having coffee. It's a hundred degrees out here and they're having fucking coffee."

They are still gathered around the door, now watching us.

"Fucking morons," Napes says. He opens his *Muscle & Fitness*.

"Platoon coming in," Gleeson calls down from the tower. Napes rolls open the gate—it shudders and squeaks. Mason counts the trucks and checks the bumper number of the last in line. I mark it on the log.

Napes picks up his magazine. Mason picks up his book, but hesitates. "It's not just coffee," he says. "Nahla is reading their fortunes in the grounds."

"Nahla?" I say.

"Yeah, the one in Western clothes." Only one woman is not in some form of head covering. She's wearing jeans and a red T-shirt, and pouring from a silver urn.

"Fortune?" Napes says. "She thinks she can see the future?"

"She does," Mason says. "But don't go over there."

"Why not?"

Mason, looking into his book, says, "Because you're in Baghdad. Nothing she can tell you about your future is going to be good. Best case—you live."

"Shit," Napes says, "that's enough." He walks back to the shed. Nahla begins moving inside.

"Wait, wait," Napes says. Nahla looks up at him. She has dark, shoulder-length hair, brown eyes, a skinny frame with a round face, about thirty years old. "Fortune?" he says.

She looks down at the silver tray covered in cups and saucers with the urn in the center. "No," she says. "No fortunes."

"Come on, I know that you can read the coffee grounds or whatever. Read me my fortune."

When Napes returns to his chair Mason says, "She going to do it?"

"Yeah."

"That's sweet of her."

"Fuck, sweet? She charged me twenty bucks."

A few minutes later Nahla brings Napes a cup and saucer. They are tiny in his hands. Fragile white. He sits forward in his chair, his M-4 hanging from his shoulder by its buttstock. His barrel hits the ground. He takes a very serious sip.

"Bring me the cup when only grounds are left," Nahla says.

"How is it?" I ask.

"It's good," he says. "You should have her read yours." Nahla looks at me, then at Mason, and turns away. I look to the base of the guard tower across the FOB, try to see where the fifty-cal round impacted an hour ago. I wonder how much lower it might have landed had it first gone through me. Dinner chow is still hours away and the thought of hot coffee tightens my stomach around the little baklava left, whatever wasn't puked up earlier. I sip water, still looking for that bullet.

Nahla goes into the shed. Napes drinks. "Careful," Mason says, "take your time. You want her to be able to read the grounds right, don't you?" Napes stops mid-sip. Mason follows her into the shed. Napes swallows. He's staring at his small cup. His barrel is still sitting in dirt.

"Sergeant Mills," Mason says from the doorway of the shed. "Check this out."

Inside, the shed is spare. Bare wooden walls. No windows. A turned-off lamp hanging from the peaked ceiling, an unlined garbage can, metal folding chairs in one corner. Daylight floods in through the doorway. Along the back wall is a small wooden table topped with the silver tray and coffee service, water bottles, additional cups and saucers, a couple pots, and a hot plate. Nahla hands me a cup and saucer. She smiles.

"Ever had the local coffee?" Mason says.

"No." The cup is small in my hands too, but feels weighty. "I don't know—"

"Just coffee, no fortune," Nahla says. "Is good." Mason sips from his cup. I look into mine. It's black and steaming. When I drink it burns my tongue. I suck coffee from my top lip. Its sweetness sits in my mouth—it won't be swallowed.

"Thank you," I say. "It's delicious." Out the door Napes is still working intently, taking serious pulls from his cup. Mason and Nahla talk quietly, friendly. I drink. It goes fast. At the bottom there is a ring of nothing around the base with a disk of blackness in the center. On the side that I drank from is a trail of grounds leading up to the rim. Somewhere in it, in the darkness, is the story of my death. Of the how and when, maybe even the why. The when is the thing, though. I want there to be a tomorrow for me in the bottom of this tiny cup.

Nahla and Mason are laughing softly. There are tears in my eyes, but I'm not crying. I don't know how to ask.

"So," I say, "is this all bullshit?" I don't look away from my cup. They stop laughing. Nahla steps close to me. I feel a tear on the cusp of falling—I am willing it not to. Nahla begins to speak, but the tear drops, streaking down my cheek. Mason looks away, to nowhere, to a corner away from me. I brush my face with my sleeve. "I'm sorry," I say.

She takes the cup and saucer from my hand. She smiles again. "It is not bullshit, it is coffee. For you it is for drinking. For me it is for reading. That is all."

Mason turns back and hands his cup to her. Both his hands are holding the saucer. When she takes it, she uses both her hands. "Shukran," he says.

"You are welcome," Nahla says. She adds them to the table.

"She doesn't read for soldiers," Mason says. "It's bad juju, like I told Napes. No news is good news."

"What about Napes?" I say.

"He is asshole," Nahla says. "He calls me Hajji. I take his money, and give him coffee. That is all."

Mason and I head to our chairs. Napes passes us holding his cup and saucer in one hand, his thumb stretched over the cup, tiny in his lean, tan fingers. Mason picks up his book. I stare at Napes's back in the open doorway and picture the grounds I left unread. My eyes sting slightly. I blink. I look at the inside of the gate. Blue paint and or-ange metal, all peeling and rust.

When Napes comes back he's shaking his head. Nahla is standing inside, smiling down at an empty cup.

"What's the verdict?" Mason says without looking up.

"Shit," Napes says. "Bunch of bullshit." My stomach growls a little and cramps a little. I drink half a bottle of water before I have to stop to breathe.

"Bad news?" Mason says. Nahla walks into the shed, out of sight. "Are you a marked man? If you're set to die some-time soon, Mills should ask to be taken off your fucking truck."

Napes sits, his rifle *thunks* into the dirt. He laughs a little, to himself, into his hands, then harder, until his eyes are red and glossed. He wipes his face on his sleeve. Starts to laugh but clenches his jaw until it passes. "I ain't dying," he says, "Worse. She says I have leave coming up. Says I'm going to meet my future wife. That I'm going to come back fucking engaged." Napes starts bouncing a knee.

Burnside, Sawyer, Doc, and Alvarez walk up. "We're here to relieve you shit-bags," Sawyer says. "Alvarez, up in the tower." Alvarez starts climbing the ladder.

"Did I hear that right?" Burnside says. "You getting mar-ried, Napes? That's some shit. Congratulations."

V IS FOR VALOR

The v-device is worn to denote acts of heroism involving conflict with an armed enemy.

You're on patrol. You have two choices: keep your eyes open and your mouth shut, move through the sector like a professional soldier, and sleep like a baby at the end of the day; or act like a fucking idiot.

You choose the latter: That was the trick, you say, he just stood there and let people shoot him. With their own guns and everything.

Uh huh, Gleeson says.

His jacket, you say, was packed with glass. Way back then and he basically invented Kevlar.

The buildings are close together and the street is packed with locals. The intel is that the Mahdi are somewhere around. Too many people to get trucks through, so you're on foot.

He made his living, you say, just letting folks shoot him. And shouldn't that be enough? A fella comes into town, charges you two bits, and you get to shoot him right in the chest. And he doesn't die. He gets back up.

Do you ever shut the fuck up? Mason says.

The sun is off to the side, the whole patrol is in shadow. You see a flash of green down an alleyway.

You have two choices: report that you might have seen a Mahdi in uniform, you know, the green and black that the ROE says to shoot on sight; or keep running your mouth.

You choose: It wasn't enough, you say. Some bastard shoots him right in the dick. Watches him die looking surprised as fuck.

No shit, Gleeson says. He's an idiot and deserved to get dick-shot. I'm glad he's dead. If he were here right now, I'd shoot him in the dick. Now seriously, no more fucking stories.

Contact, contact! Mason says. RPG! Three o'clock!

The rocket screams past, two meters behind you, explodes into the wheel well of a bongo truck. The patrol goes flat on the sidewalk, the locals run over each other in all directions. The bongo truck smokes.

On me, Sergeant Mills says.

Your crew stacks at the edge of the alley. AK fire erupts from the gaggle of green and black.

You have two choices: wait for the command, move-to-contact together, and overwhelm the enemy the way you've been trained to; or fall out of the stack in a panic, ignore the sensation of piss soaking clear through your uniform, and send unaimed bullets down the alley.

Go, Mills says.

You are already two steps outside the stack but they are rolling forward faster than you are fucking up. You clear the corner and your M-4 is up and going. You jerk your trigger *ta-ta-tat*, *ta-ta-tat*. The alley is long and bent. Rounds impact at your feet, against the walls. You don't see shit. You move forward. You keep shooting.

The patrol is holding their formation, moving down the alley as a fire-team. They cover each other as they reload. They take cover in the debris that lines the walls. Except for you. The moving forward makes you feel better, pulling the trigger calms you down. At the end of the magazine you realize you're too far out in front and alone on your side of the street. You reload behind a dumpster, thumb your selector switch from BURST to SEMI, like you're about to be more thoughtful in your shooting.

The second RPG sucks past. Blasts into the smoking bongo truck.

Back to BURST.

Fall back, Mills says.

You have two choices: follow your goddamn orders, fall back to the main drag, call up the QRF to bring in some trucks; or run into the dark of that alleyway blasting away all by yourself so that your entire patrol has to chase after you.

Leaning out from your dumpster, you squeeze three even pulls, *ta-ta-tat*, *ta-ta-tat*, *ta-ta-tat*. Then you start running. Forward.

You can't hear—that went with the first blast and has only gotten worse. You make it to the bend in the alley before you realize the AK fire has died out.

On three, you tell yourself. On three you'll round the corner.

You make it to two when the green and blacks run smack into you. They have a third RPG ready to send down to the rest of the patrol. You level your M-4, a burst into the first chest. A mad scramble to fire off the RPG. *Ta-ta-tat* into the second chest. Orange backblast engulfs the narrow walls. The Mahdi stands there, launcher on shoulder, hands on grips, watching the grenade fly. He's so close you can touch him with the end of your barrel. You do, you press it firmly against his chest. *Boom*, you think you hear. *Ta-ta-tat*.

Behind you there is only smoke. You peek around the corner, don't see shit, and fire two bursts down it anyway. Gleeson scares the shit out of you, hitting you on the shoulder. Back to the road, he says. QRF is coming.

I got them, you say. I got all three.

You're a fucking idiot, Gleeson says. You follow him into the smoke.

At the open mouth of the alleyway, two men are pulling security. Gleeson turns off and points his rifle back at the bend in the alley—at the three dead Mahdi. Mills and the rest of the patrol are hurriedly picking up what used to be the left arm of Private Alvarez, who is sitting against the wall, looking at where his shoulder is supposed to be coming out of his vest.

What the fuck? you say.

Help with Alvarez, Mills says.

You have two choices: take a knee, apply pressure, hold in the blood until QRF arrives; or finish pissing.

As the last drop runs down your thigh, gathers above where your kneepads cinch tight, you fall onto both knees, let your rifle clank into the bloody ground. You push your hands into the opening of the vest, into shoulder meat. Blood runs over. You take the compress out of a front pocket of Alverez's vest, push that into the wound. Blood runs out the sides and down.

Gleeson fires a few rounds. Movement, he says.

Mills tells you to secure the alley, to stay with Gleeson.

What about Alvarez? you say.

Don't you worry about Alvarez, Mason says.

No, Gleeson says, let him work on Alvarez. Let him clean up his mess.

Alvarez's eyes are open and downcast, looking past his wound. Mills says, He was dead the second he was hit. You continue to hold onto that compress, listening to Gleeson fire. It's slow, measured. There is no AK fire coming back. You hold on to Alvarez.

Trucks are here, Mills says. Get him to the trucks.

You hold on to Alvarez.

Get up—get him to the fucking trucks.

You pull the compress away. You take the compress from your vest-front and push it into the wound.

Get the fuck up, Mills says.

You push and push and push.

Mills taps hard three times on the back of your Kevlar. You turn in time to see the butt of his rifle coming down, smashing into your face and exploding your nose.

Your patrol drags you and Alvarez to the humvees, puts you in the same seat in two different trucks—the casualty seat—and puts your rifle at your feet. At Alvarez's feet, they put what's left of his arm.

They bring you and Alvarez here to the CASH.

They leave you here so the docs can make sense of your face. And do the paperwork on Alvarez.

You have two choices: sign the statement saying you got separated from the patrol by the second RPG; you aggressed alone, heroically, single-handedly killing those responsible for the attack that lead to the death of Private Alvarez; receive the Bronze Star with V device for your effort, a Purple Heart too for that broken nose you sustained in the skirmish; Or don't sign it, Alvarez will fly home with the story of how he died as a direct result of your actions pinned to his coffin, and your platoon will undoubtedly find a way to frag you the next time you leave the wire.

No, shut your fucking mouth. What you have to say is about as useful as Private Alvarez's left hand.

You have one choice: sign the statement.

Sign it. Sign the goddamn statement. Sign it, do you understand me? Private Napes?

"Yes, sir."

Matty,

You know this is not our story, right? Please
find your own story, a true story, and write that.
Write about Justin. Write about sitting around
the front gate. Write about sitting in a guard tower all damn day. Write about something else.

Do fucking better.

Stone

THE RIFLE

I

Another combat patrol. We slink our string of trucks through busy turnarounds, jammed with traffic. Horns sounding off in all directions. Turn off onto smaller side streets, full of vendors and shoppers. In narrow residential neighborhoods, our gunners have to duck to get under all the wires and cables the Iraqis have strung up. Because we're last in line our gunner, Gleeson, faces backwards, wagging his fifty-cal over the back hatch of the truck. "Duck," Hicks says to him from the front right seat. Gleeson drops down in the turret, the low sag of wires missing his Kevlar by half a meter.

"When I get home on leave I'm gonna tear shit up," Napes says from the driver's seat.

"Anyone in particular?" Hicks says.

"Well, first my girlfriend, then I'm open to suggestions." They both laugh. "What about you, Sergeant?"

"Oh, well, you know," Hicks says. He taps the gold band

of his wedding ring against the stock of his M-4. "I'm sure I'll tear my fair share up."

Out my window, the brown of it all slides past. I sit in the back left seat. Behind Napes. Always.

"I've been setting it all up," Napes says. "Emailed all my old girlfriends, told how I was in Baghdad and did they have any sympathy for a lonely soldier."

"Yeah?" Hicks says.

"Turns out, they all do."

From the turret, Gleeson calls down, "Hey, Little Bird."

"Man, stop calling me that."

"No. I like it. It suits you. It's what you sound like."

"Fuck you," Napes says.

"Fuck me? You'd love that, wouldn't you, Little Bird? Alright, alright, I'll let you throw one in me but it has to be before you hit leave. I'm not cool with following *all* those girlfriends of yours."

Napes sits quiet.

"Unless you mean fuck me in the fucked forever sense, like the way you fucked Alvarez."

Napes sits.

"Is that what you meant, Little Bird? Fuck me like you fucked Alvarez?"

"That's enough," Hicks says.

Napes is driving, both hands on the wheel. I can't see his face and he's gone quiet. He follows the truck in front of us as we turn onto a wide-open, four-lane street.

Crowds pack the sidewalks, overflowing the curbs. Traffic veers. Vendors lean over smoking grills. Men hold hands, strolling slowly, smiling; well-covered women walk in quiet clusters. Children run and laugh and scream like kids back home.

And then, they slowly fall away.

The road continues, the buildings, the sidewalk, the garbage, but the people are caught behind doorways and the cusps of alleyways, peeking over the sills of their taped-up windows.

Out in front of us, from within a newly patched piece of road, light and dirt and concrete explode:

My atoms separate, expand, lose their bonding, intermingle with atoms belonging to other structures that have also expanded, time stops, not gradually but instantly, stops, existence utterly pauses, having first been blown apart.

For an instant the moment hangs, frozen, followed by an inkling of what's to come, an easing of the stillness back into movement, then a violent coming together of atomic particles back into their principal forms, but with such force that the remnants are left shaken—vibrating.

I slam back together, back into existence, and into the thick brown of the falling dust cloud. I thought it would be fire and heat but we roll through and it's a mouth full of dust. Sound is a solid tone, a beep that not quite covers the *fuck fuck fuck* that Napes is chanting. And then, the *ka-ka-ka* of AK fire. The four crew-served machine guns sing back. I look ahead through the cracked windshield. Our trucks are driving forward. Next to me, Gleeson's legs shake, from fear and from the kicking of his fifty-cal. Hot brass falls like rain through his feet. I set my hand on his knee; it settles some. He fires less. I move my hand back to my rifle. Napes accelerates and Gleeson stops firing.

The radio cracks. Hicks yells into his hand-mic, "I-E-D, over."

"Improvised my fucking ass," Gleeson calls down. "Somebody's been practicing."

"Fuck…fuck…fuck…" Napes goes on.

Our line of trucks stops after 300 meters. "Dismounts out," the radio says. I get out. I scan the road all the way to the sidewalk, begin scanning the buildings.

Gleeson pushes links and brass from where they collected on top of the turret until they slide down the sides of the humvee. He scans over the sights of his fifty-cal. "Mills, look," he says. The blast area is no longer vacant, the street is flooded with dancing locals, waving arms, smiling toothy smiles. Some of the men have their cocks out, wagging them at us.

I hear more now—Napes saying *fuck* real quiet—AK fire petering out behind us.

Three boys begin throwing rocks from an alley on my side of the humvee. One the size of my fist slams into my door. "Fuck!" Napes says.

I pick up the rock and throw it as hard as I can. "Fuck you!" I say. It sails past them and thuds. They're laughing, gathering more stones.

"Napes, get in the fucking turret," Gleeson says. "Hurry up, I have to piss."

"What? No," Napes says. "We just drove through an IED, there's no fucking way."

Gleeson climbs out of the turret, jumps down onto the hood, and then onto the street. We have no gunner. I start to climb up. "Hold it Mills," Hicks says. "Private Napes, you have until I hear urine hitting sidewalk to get your ass in that turret or you'll goddamn walk back to the FOB. You are all done ignoring orders. You've ignored too many lately. Now move."

Napes steps out of the truck, rifle in hand. He climbs up the hood and drops into the turret. Gleeson walks between Napes's open door and the truck frame, begins pissing.

BANG.

One shot, loud and close. From above and behind me. I turn in time to see Napes slump in the turret. Gleeson jumps half into the driver's seat, jerks the humvee forward a few feet, then slams on the brakes. I run toward the truck. Hicks calls out, "Mount up!" Napes sinks down into the truck, slow like drowning. The truck jerks forward again. Something long and black slides over the top and down the long slope of the back hatch, clatters onto the street—Napes's M-4.

In the dust of the moving vehicle I pick up the rifle and sprint after my truck. Gleeson slams on the brakes and I get in. I shove the rifle behind my seat-back, behind the ammo cans, and stick the barrel of my own rifle out my window. "Fucking go!" Hicks says.

The truck jumps forward and Napes tries to fall. His vest is caught on the turret strap. His hand is pushing against the hole in his neck but the blood is pushing harder.

"Is he dead?" Gleeson says. "Is he fucking dead?"

Hicks and I pry the strap loose from his vest bottom and Napes crumbles onto the gunner's platform. Hicks is turned around, pushing Napes into the back seat. "Get behind the fucking gun," he says. He has both hands around Napes's throat, blood coming out between his fingers. I climb up and grab the handles of the fifty-cal. There's blood all over the turret.

"Fuck," Gleeson says. "Fuck…fuck…"

Through the main gate the first three trucks pull off at the clearing barrels. We tear around them toward the medics' rooms. Gleeson stops the humvee and I climb out of the top of the turret. Two medics beat me to Napes's door.

They drag him out and into their building, Hicks covered in blood, me standing in dust.

Top and The Commander come running up. "Where?" the CO says. Hicks points at the medics' door. The wind pulls a bloody wisp from the end of his finger. The CO crashes through, slams the door behind him. Hicks is staring at his wisp.

"Get that truck to the motor pool," Top says.

"I ain't leaving," Hicks says.

"You're a fucking mess. Take the truck back, change your uniform. You're not doing anybody any good like that."

Hicks wipes his hand on his thigh. It takes a lot of wiping. "As soon as we have word," he says, "I'll change. Not a goddamn second before."

Top steps close to Hicks, looks down at him. The growl starts before the words, "Now you listen here—"

"I'll kill you," Hicks says. He's staring at his hands, fingers curled in, half-circles of blood drying like nail polish. His voice is matter-of-fact. "One more word and I'll slit your useless throat in your sleep." Top slack-jaw-stares, but doesn't make words. To me, Hicks says, "You heard the First Sergeant, get this truck to the motor pool. Then come back."

I walk around to my door, run my finger along the mark left by the fist-size stone, and get in. Gleeson drives us over and parks. He leaves without a word.

As soon as I'm alone, I reach back and pull Napes's rifle out. Where I grab, halfway down the stock, is sticky. I hold it, like it's my own, transferring blood to the handgrip, squeezing it until it stops shaking—until I stop shaking.

I get out and check the motor pool for people. Everyone's gone. I take his rifle into my room. The door opens onto the foot of my bunk, laundry bag hanging from a crossbar. Mine has a top bunk where my roommate, Sawyer, and I keep our extra duffle bags. At the head of my bed is the only window, blurry Plexiglas, the bottom half of which has been replaced by an air conditioner that Sawyer always sets too fucking cold. Next to that is my bookshelf. Sawyer's bunk sits to the other side of the doorway. It's made up perfectly.

I go to my bunk. Blood and all, I tuck Napes's rifle under my blanket and sheets. I pull them up, smooth out the edges. Like a sleeping baby.

I take my own rifle out into the motor pool. Our platoon's trucks are parked along our wall of Hesco barriers but they are crooked, frantic-looking next to the adjacent rows of perfectly parked humvees. Joes from the other platoons are coming out of the barracks, pointing their scared faces at me. A few ask what happened. I open and close my fist, sticky with Napes's blood. When they see this, they start running out of the motor pool, toward the medic station. I am alone in the dust and gravel. The wind has died. The sky sits over all of it, a clear blue that turns brown at the horizon.

"Little Bird," I answer. "They killed Little Bird."

I start running.

II

What I see outside the medic station is worse than watching Napes slump. The whole company, everyone who isn't out on a mission, is crying their fucking guts out. Men

I've known for years, some whose hands I've never shaken, some whose homes I've gotten drunk in, some who attended my wedding, are screaming themselves hoarse. Everyone is red-faced. Tears and snot on everything.

I cry too, bent over, elbows on my knees. Between sobs, I retch, like I can't get the hurt out fast enough, until I puke out water. Hicks has blood all down his front. Dust sticking to the wetness. Like he's bleeding mud. I retch again.

Beyond the square courtyard are rows of palm trees. The fronds are still. The air is quiet. Nothing moves. The world stands starkly still.

And slowly, as if the sadness really is leaving us the harder we cry, we all start crying less. Some people begin talking. Other platoons, again, ask what happened.

I run my sleeve across my face and it comes off wet. People are hugging me, my hand still sticky with Napes's blood.

Gleeson says, "He just fell. We drive through an IED, start pulling security, and he just falls. I'm trying to catch him and get him down, but he's caught on the turret strap. He's just leaned over, bleeding down on everything. I tried to see his face and where the bullet hit—"

Everyone he's talking to turns away. Burnside, all six-feet and 200-muscular-pounds of him, sits down in the new space, and cries. "Why was he in the turret?" he says. "Why the fuck was he in the turret?"

Gleeson says nothing.

Mason finds me, puts an arm around me. He half points his rifle at the closed door, now guarded by five soldiers from Headquarters Platoon. "Kurtzson tried to get in," Mason says. "First Sergeant cleared the room of everybody but medics and posted that crew to keep us out."

Kurtzson is standing a few feet from the door, facing it with his rifle at the low-ready, looking like he's just waiting to start shooting.

"What's he waiting for?" I ask.

"Same as us," Mason says. "To see the body."

It's late afternoon and the sky is turning orange, on its way to red. The heat is letting up some and the crying continues to die down. After a half-hour people start sitting down against the walls of the courtyard—nobody from our platoon, but eventually most everyone else.

The door opens. Kurtzson raises his rifle a few inches. Top walks out slow, looking first at his guards as they back away, and then at Hicks's bloody uniform. Kurtzson drops his barrel. Medics leave the room, slipping past Top, past our broke-down company.

"Two at a time," Top says. Kurtzson goes in, followed by Hicks. The door closes.

We wait.

They come out, looking worse than before. Hicks is gaunt and red. He looks empty. Kurtzson walks him back toward our motor pool.

Two more go in. And so on. Through seventy fucking men, I wait with Mason, until it's us who go in next.

The room is dark, even though floor to ceiling is painted white. Three silver tables are lined up along the wall. A long black bag lies on the center table. Mason and I stand at the foot of it. Across the top, written is what looks like white Sharpie: NAPES. It's unzipped and pulled open, but the table is so tall all I see over the bag is a tuft of hair and a glimpse of forehead. I look around and see for the first time the Commander standing in the corner behind me, opposite the door. Just standing. Watching every one of his troops view the body—like a penance. Mason steps forward, lays his hand on the bulge of Napes's feet, squeezing them through the thick bag.

I expect to smell something, but there's nothing. Just coldness. I try to step forward but my feet are stuck to the floor—not adhesively, they just won't lift. I reach out a hand, trying to touch Napes's feet but I'm so fucking scared that I might reach them, feel them, be haunted the rest of my fucking life by the feeling of those dead feet that I just fold. My elbows hit my knees and I manage to turn away, toward the door. My eyes are already wetted over, my blinking splashes tears out and onto the floor.

Mason grabs me by the shoulders and lifts me back to standing. He turns me square to the body. We move forward. Toward the body. I look down and what I see is gray and transparent. I tell myself it's the shitty light. I look down, to the bag, to the bulge of his feet. I grab his foot with my hand, my rifle still in the other, and I lean down. Mason's hand is on my shoulder.

I push my face, wet and slick, against the bag until I feel his gravity through it. I push until his density pushes back. And I sob. I don't know what else to do. I want to sob him back to life. I want to have climbed into that goddamn turret.

I look at his face. His eyes aren't fully closed. Maybe they were earlier, but now they are bulging and swollen. They're pointed up at the ceiling. His mouth is open too. Blood coagulated on his lips—black and maroon. Thick looking. Below the gray of everything is a blueness.

Mason and I wait. Keep waiting. But this room is empty. There's nothing here I've ever known.

III

Sergeant Kurtzson is waiting at the barracks door. He stops every soldier in our platoon as we pass. "If your uniforms are bloody, go change and hand them in. If your gear is bloody, get it to the hallway and start cleaning."

I walk past and go into my room. Sawyer is sitting on his bunk, just looking off.

I sit at the foot of my bunk, far enough down that I don't sit on Napes's rifle. I start breaking apart my M-4.

Sawyer looks at me. "It's this or I help clean blood off other guys' shit," I say.

He nods. Eventually he begins breaking apart his rifle too.

I'm trying not to think about blood soaking into my pillow.

From under my bunk, I retrieve a two-forty-bravo ammo can and open it. I remove rags, a bottle of CLP, and my cleaning kit.

I wipe down the outside of my rifle, only dust until I get to the bloody handgrip. I drop the guts onto my bedcover. I run a bore-brush down the barrel. It's already clean from lack of shooting. I keep an eye on Sawyer, making sure I do whatever he's doing, just a few minutes longer than him. By the time he slaps his bolt assembly into place and snaps his lower and upper receivers together, I'm still pretending to look for my cotter pin. He leaves.

I put my rifle together and slide it under my bunk.

Carefully, like removing a bandage from a burn, I roll my bedding down and away from Napes's rifle. I get an undershirt from my footlocker, cut it into strips with my

Leatherman, and begin cleaning the outside. My hands shake, they slip off the shirt and smear themselves bloody. I take a toothbrush to the handgrip, really getting into the diamond-shaped crevices. I get a bottle of water from the hallway ice-chest to rinse the bristles before taking it to the shoulder strap, which has been soaking for hours now. I give up and remove the strap, burying it in my laundry bag. I place the strap-keepers in my ammo can. *Tink tink.* It's one of the first sounds I recognize as sound since the blast.

I open up the upper and lower receivers of Napes's rifle to get at its sacred, internal pieces. I run my fingers over the charging handle, gently pull, and the bolt assembly slides free. I pull out the retaining pin, the firing pin comes loose. Rotate and pull the bolt cam pin, out falls the bolt. Every time I pull, something comes apart. I lay them out in an array, smallest to largest, all of it shades of gray. Everything is clean. Napes took care of his rifle.

Sawyer comes back in, sits roughly on his bunk. "Jesus, still working on that?" he says.

"Yep," I say, sliding the heel of my boot along my bed frame, hoping my rifle is out of sight. "Not sure what else to do."

"Well, whatever you do, don't go outside. Kurtzson has Gleeson and Burnside cleaning your fucking truck. He and Hicks, just standing back watching. Running through the sensitive-items list or some shit."

I reassemble. I add a few drops of CLP to the outside, to the metal parts, and wipe it down with one of the non-bloody rags. I push everything into the ammo can, snap it shut, and push it under my bunk too. I should have switched weapons before Sawyer got back.

I walk with Napes's rifle out into the motor pool. I see Kurtzson and Hicks looking at a notebook, shaking their heads. Gleeson is at the rear passenger window, pouring something onto the gunner's platform, his jaw set and brow squeezed white. He scrubs like he's trying to get out through the bottom of the truck. Burnside is on top, on his knees, running a cloth around the turret, pulling it away every now and again, and I see that it's red.

After Gleeson finishes below, he comes around and starts in on the floorboard of the right-rear passenger seat, where Napes's body rode back to base. Burnside jumps down onto the platform. He begins rotating the turret. Slowly at first, then faster. As he picks up speed he slaps the lock into place, slamming the turret stopped with phenomenal force. The barrel of the fifty-cal swings wild and he has to hold one of the handles to control it. But he doesn't stop. Left and right. Right and left. Unlock—*slam!* Unlock—*slam!* Harder and harder until Kurtzson screams at him to stop.

He locks the turret and looks down at all of us. Gleeson standing closest, bloody rags in hand, just gawks at Burnside's ability to convey rage.

"Why was Napes in the turret?" he says, and turns away.

Kurtzson looks back at the notepad. He says, "And you checked everywhere? In the hatch? Everywhere?"

"Yeah, I looked. I had Gleeson look—the rifle's fucking gone," Hicks says.

"Alright, I'll go tell The Commander."

I go back inside before he passes me. In my room, Sawyer is gone. I sit on my bunk.

I pull the covers up, over the small streaks of blood, and lie down. I hold the rifle, pull it into my chest, feel the texture of the handgrip, reach my trigger finger out, past the trigger guard, I rest it on the magazine release. I feel the circular pattern of it, I stroke it as I have my own rifle, I push it in, hold it, release it, and look at the pattern it leaves on my finger-pad. I wonder if Napes ever had such an imprint, if he ever pressed hard enough. I feel a cry coming on.

There's a loud knock on my door.

"What?" I say, not getting up.

The door opens and Gleeson sticks his head in. "Meet up with Sergeant Hicks," he says. "Every truck is doing a sensitive-items check." He leaves.

I hold Napes's rifle for a few more minutes. I separate the upper receiver from the lower receiver and bury them in my laundry bag. From the outside, I can make out the shape of the carrying handle and front sight post. I remove the upper receiver and put it on my shelf, behind the row of books.

This is a terrible idea, I think.

IV

"Did I give you a copy of our crew's sensitive-items list?" Hicks asks.

"No, but I have one," I say.

He's looking at his map board. There are pages clipped to it, but no sensitive-items list.

"Grab Gleeson and run through everything. Let me know ASAP."

"Should we start with yours?"

"My what?"

"Do you want to give me your numbers now," I say, "or after I finish with Gleeson, and the truck?"

He looks up from his board. His eyes are red, darting around my face, but not landing. "Oh, yeah, come by my room when you're finished. We can check my gear last."

"Roger," I say.

"Oh, and Napes's gear too," Hicks says.

I get my list from my room and find Gleeson in the junior enlisted room. "Grab your shit and meet me at the truck."

"Fuck," Gleeson says.

Mason is holding a book, sitting on his bunk. Not reading, just holding. "I need your help with Napes's sensitive-items," I say. "Can you bring everything you can find in his room to our truck?"

"Roger," Mason says. I'm already walking out into the motor pool.

Mason comes out first. "There's nothing in his room," he says. "No vest, no Kevlar, no rifle." He opens the back hatch and pulls out Napes's night-vision goggles. By the time Gleeson drags his gear to the truck, wearing none of it, actually dragging it, Mason has already confirmed the serial numbers on all the gear, fifty-cal, and radios. Assuming the helmet and vest are still with the medics, the only thing missing is Napes's rifle.

I start checking Gleeson's numbers. "Burnside's blaming me," he says. "Keeps asking why Napes was in the turret." I don't say anything. "Like it's my fucking fault. Like no other gunner has ever had their driver cover them while they pissed."

"Nods," I say.

"What?"

"Nods, where's your night vision?"

He slams them onto the hood of the truck. "Right fucking here. Are you listening to me? Burnside thinks it's my fucking fault. Like it wouldn't have been me otherwise. Or you. Like it only happened because it was Napes."

"It was Napes," I say, "because we, all of us—you, me, and Hicks—put him there. And we put him there because of Alvarez." I return to the sensitive items list and Gleeson doesn't say anything except serial numbers until we're through. Mason just watches.

When everything checks out, I send them back to their room to continue grieving. Alone with the truck, I sit in my dismount seat and close the door. I look up through the open turret to where I see Gleeson gunning when we roll out. I see him scanning over his fifty-cal. He's shaking his fist at cars. He's throwing candy to kids. I hear them scream, "Chalk-o-lot, chalk-o-lot!" They're smiling. They scramble in the street to pick it up. When I look back, Napes is in the turret. He's too small for it, like he's playing army, Kevlar sitting back on his head, slender bird neck coming up from his vest. And I see him slump. Fall forward and hesitate, like he might just stand back up. He falls through the turret and he's fucking dead.

I'm hunched forward, sobbing. I drop my rifle barrel-first onto the floorboard, feel it bang against my knee, and take the chair-back in both hands. I can't push against it hard enough. I'm shaking, my eyes are squeezed shut, I feel the truck take my grief. It shakes too, but not enough.

There's a knock on my window. I jump. Kurtzson is looking around the motor pool like he hadn't just seen me weeping. I wipe my face with both hands, wipe both hands on my pants, and open the door.

"Sergeant Mills, is everything okay out here?"

"Yes, Sergeant. I was just finishing the sensitive-items check for our crew."

Kurtzson stops pretending to look around. "Sergeant Hicks isn't checking your shit?"

"No, Sergeant. He asked me to do it. I only have his gear left."

"Everything accounted for?"

"Napes's rifle is missing."

His face doesn't change. I'm not sure if he's ever going to blink again. "Where did Napes keep his rifle during missions?"

"Depends. In the gun-rack by the driver's seat usually. But he was relieving Gleeson in the turret. Could have taken it up there with him. Or it could have fallen out of the rack—the door was still open when we started to roll."

Kurtzson breathes in and holds. Behind his sunglasses I think his eyes might be shut. Finally, "Carry on."

Hicks is sitting on his bunk. "Where are we at?"

"Napes's rifle isn't in his room or on the truck. We must have left it where we pulled security. Only your gear is left."

"Okay, well I'll check my shit. No need to waste any-more of your time." I hand him the list. "Sergeant Mills?" The list is shaking in his hands. "I checked bunks while you were in the motor pool."

I don't move. Eyes don't blink. Muscles don't twitch. I am stone. My heart kicks blood up into my face so hard I can't quite make out Hicks sitting in front of me. I'm dizzy and I need to shit. "Oh yeah?"

"Yeah." He looks up at me. His eyes are crying, but nothing else about him is. "There's blood in your bed."

I really think I'm going to shit myself in this sad man's small room. His face is pleading. He just wants to not know there's blood in my bed. "Is there anything else in my room?"

He looks down to the list. "Nothing that I found. Is there anything you should tell me?"

"I'll be sure to have my sheets washed."

Alone in my room, I stare down at my bunk. I lean my rifle against the bed-frame and in one huge pull, remove my blanket and sheets from my mattress. I roll them so that the green blanket stays on the outside of the bundle. I pry open my laundry bag and begin to shove. I find half of Napes's rifle. It's only been buried for two hours. Napes has been dead for less than six.

I take the piece of cold metal and put it with the other half of the rifle, behind my row of books.

I think about taking the bag to the laundry building but decide that that would be an excellent way to get caught with Napes's rifle. Instead I dig my sleeping bag out of my duffle bag and throw it haphazardly across my mattress, like I've been sleeping in it for days.

I lie down. I close my eyes. I see Napes slump. I open my eyes. I do that until dinner chow, through dinner chow, until nightfall, and goddamn sun-up.

V

Private First Class Napes died yesterday. At breakfast chow I sit in front of a plate of scrambled eggs and buttered toast that makes me nauseous. Gleeson is the only soldier from our platoon with a goddamn appetite. I throw my food away and go back to the barracks.

Outside the door to the motor pool, Mason is waiting for me. "Did you just get breakfast?" he says.

"I tried. I went, got food, sat down, and realized what I was doing. I think I'm on autopilot."

"There's a funeral." His eyes are wide like he's asking a question.

"When?"

"Noon."

"Seems soon," I say.

Mason smiles like he's chewing back vomit. "I was listening in at the TOC. We're still on missions. We roll this afternoon."

"Jesus." My stomach is empty except for water. I feel my cheek, I need to shave. I thought the war would take a day off.

The door swings open and Hicks comes out. He looks from Mason to me. In his face, I see my bloody sheets. He walks past. From several meters away he calls back, "Tell the men, formation at eleven-thirty. We're going over to see the Chaplain."

Mason and I go to our respective rooms. I sit on my bunk, staring at my bookshelf. Sawyer is in his bed, writing a letter home. Our phone and internet privileges have been suspended, pending notification of Napes's family.

"Did you go to breakfast?" he says.

"I tried. I needed something to do. Funeral's at noon. Formation at eleven-thirty."

"Shit," he says. He puts his paper and pen down. "I'll go tell the platoon." He leaves.

I gather up my bag of bloody sheets and take it to the laundry building.

At noon our platoon is standing in the motor pool, as are first, second, fourth, and headquarters platoons. The Commander and Top come out. "What the fuck?" Top says. "Form up!" Seventy men just look at him. "Form. Up. Now."

We slowly and ineptly gather ourselves into five groups, roughly arranged around where he's standing.

"Fuck it," the CO says. Then louder, "Alright men, we're walking over to the church. Stay in formation. Let's go."

And we start walking.

It's quiet. The sun's above us and even without our ger it's getting hot. Maybe 110 degrees. When we come out of the motor pool we see them. The other three Cavalry companies standing around, a hundred men each, outside the chow hall, their barracks, watching us walk to our funeral. A jagged line of faces and uniforms and rifles, on both sides as we go. Some nod as we pass, a tight gesture of condolence. Most are statues with their shoulders rolled forward and their faces downcast. Not their eyes, though. Their eyes are watching. They want to know, for when it happens to them. Alvarez never left the CASH, so no funeral. And he was a backfill. He died unknown and his death was mostly unseen. Napes is the first real casualty in full view of the battalion. So they watch.

It feels like shit. Being looked at.

The chapel is a few hundred meters away, it takes forever to get there. The sky is cloudless and huge above us. It's so still we might be marching underwater. It feels that thick.

When we get there, the CO says, "Stop."

We do.

"Right face," he says, but not in a serious way.

We turn. The Chaplain is standing next to the door of the light brown building. I think about walking back to my bunk and waiting this out.

The Commander and Top talk to the Chaplain and tell us to fall out and find seats inside. Mason and I find two folding chairs in the back of the room. Burnside stands against the back wall. I can't find Gleeson.

An aisle bisects the rows of chairs. In front, on a raised platform, is a pair of desert boots. Sticking up from the boots is a rifle. There is a Kevlar helmet set on the stock of the M-4, a pair of dogtags dangling lightly from the handgrip.

The air-conditioner is on—it's freezing.

Who's fucking rifle is that? I try not to think about my bookshelf. I look in front of me and across the aisle. Hicks is looking back at me. I look at my hands.

The Chaplain walks to the front of the room, at the foot of the platform. "Men, yesterday we suffered a great tragedy." His voice is soft. "Private First Class Justin Napes died heroically…"

I'm done listening. I'm looking at the rifle. It isn't as clean as Napes's. I begin to breathe jagged.

The Chaplain is speaking. Time is passing. The room is freezing. Mason is sitting next to me, his knee bouncing like Gleeson's when we're taking fire. I start to reach my hand to him, but realize that outside the truck, it's different. And he's not my gunner. I let him bounce his knee.

The Chaplain stops talking and steps aside. Top walks to the front of the room. "Men, I hoped to God I'd never have to read this. To you or to anyone. But here we are."

And he reads:

> Halfway down the trail to Hell,
> In a shady meadow green,
> Are the Souls of all dead troopers camped,
> Near a good old-time canteen,
> And this eternal resting place
> Is known as Fiddlers' Green.

I've heard this before. I was drunk. We were all drunk. Some private fresh out of boot had just been awarded his Stetson for winning some award. He was stripped down to his boxers, hat, and boots, whiskey bottle in hand, really letting us have it. He shook his fist and sloshed his booze, he sang it out, the canteen that waits for us all, yellow light shining down in some barracks on his sweaty, smiling face, he let us have it, he let us have it, he made us believe, if not in it then certainly in him, he really let us have it—Gleeson, on the day he earned his Stetson.

> And so when man and horse go down
> Beneath a saber keen,
> Or in a roaring charge of fierce melee
> You stop a bullet clean,
> And the hostiles come to get your scalp,
> Just empty your canteen,
> And put your pistol to your head
> And go to Fiddlers' Green.

Top is not a good First Sergeant. He's hard about the wrong things and soft everywhere else. But he never once looked at the paper. He recited "Fiddlers' Green," tears in his eyes, without stumbling on a single word. He did his fucking job. He is a good First Sergeant today.

"Private Napes," he says, pushing the paper into his pocket, "you got there first, to the Green. Be ready for us, one day we'll join you. We are the Cavalry." He steps aside.

The Commander steps to the front. "Men, I have no words. Private Napes was a fine soldier and we won't be the same without him." He clenches his jaw and his fists and turns to the boots-Kevlar-rifle-dogtags. He salutes. He looks back. "One at a time, come up and pay your respects." He steps aside.

The aisle quickly fills with men waiting to step up, salute, and move on.

Step up. Salute. Move on.

It takes a long time for Mason and me to make our way into the aisle. After soldiers pass by the dogtags, they walk to the periphery of the room, then hit the door and evaporate. Gone. I'm standing behind Mason in line. By the time he's up and saluting, only the Chaplain, Commander, and First Sergeant are in the front half of the room. Everyone else is trying to be anywhere else.

Mason moves on. My turn.

I step up. The room is so fucking cold. I snap a salute. Put it down. I try to turn away, but can't. I stumble forward, reach out, and grab Napes's dogtags. I squeeze them in my fist and the tears come. I'm bending forward and my fist is at my lips and I'm kissing the cold chain, pressing it into my skin. Tears fall onto the back of my hand. I can't squeeze the tags hard enough.

I let them fall against the rifle. Not Napes's rifle. I stand.

I don't turn crisply, no pivot on toe and heel. I just step away. I'm not moving on, I'm just leaving.

VI

There is a kind of heat that obliterates sweat. Air so hot that sweat never actually rests on the skin—it sublimates directly from the pore into the atmosphere. I feel it, a constant giving-away of the self, leaving me with the thought—*at what point has it taken everything?*

It's two hours after Napes's funeral and this is the kind of heat we're standing in. The adjacent unit reported an IED attack on the same road we were hit on yesterday.

Outside my truck, I pull security. I pace across the dust. Near the lead truck lies the exploded hull of an armored vehicle, with holes blown through it like shotgun spread. The IED came complete with a sack of ball bearings. People died inside this vehicle.

At my feet is a dark stain. I wonder if any of it came out of Napes. I remember that we survived the explosion and I look 300 meters up the road. That's where his blood would be.

"What, were there no other units to call out here for this shit?" Gleeson says from the turret behind me. "Pretty sure nobody died here from Alpha or Bravo or Charlie yesterday."

"It's still our sector," Hicks says. He's looking out his window, not talking to either of us directly.

"I know it's our sector," Gleeson says, "just like it's Alpha and Bravo's sector. And Charlie's. It's a *battalion* sector. I'm saying, *we* were hit here yesterday. What the fuck?"

On my side of the road, there's a dead space before the buildings start. I walk toward it until the toes of my boots touch the curb. There are Xs on all the windows in wide, grayish tape. "Are we calling up things like taped-up windows?" I say. "Like, as intel?"

"This road is used all the time by Americans," Hicks says. "It's just a function of living here."

"What-the-fuck-ever," Gleeson says. "These people know what's up. They probably taped up right before the attack."

"Which attack, exactly?" Hicks says. "Today's? Yesterday's? You don't think enough shit has blown up here for them to just always have them taped?"

"Fuck that," Gleeson says. "I don't know how, but they get word. There's probably some kind of Hajji newsletter."

Between two of the closest buildings a handful of kids emerge, see us, and hang back in the shadows.

"Sergeant Mills," Hicks says. "Soccer balls."

"Roger." I walk to the back hatch, open it slightly, and retrieve three balls. They are white with a green splotch the shape of Iraq and Arabic writing I don't understand. We are supposed to hand them to children with both hands, formally, an act of significance—this giving. But I don't have it in me. From the curb I throw them in their general direction. They scamper out from the alleyway, grab the balls, and vanish.

"They throw rocks," Gleeson says, "and we give them soccer balls. Some fucking war."

I look back up the road. 300 meters. I look at the blown-out hull nearby. I hate this fucking place.

The radio cracks: "Mount up."

I get into the driver's seat.

I didn't eat last night or this morning and I'm still not hungry. I feel weak under my gear. My rifle has never felt so heavy. In the motor pool Gleeson pushes past me and heads into the barracks. I say to Mason, "Food?"

"I should eat."

We drop our gear inside the truck and take only our rifles.

The chow hall consists of a pair of trailers—one to serve and eat in, and one for storage. The entrance is at the top of some stairs where the two trailers meet. Waiting in line on the stairs I see the Battalion Commander standing with the Alpha and Charlie Company commanders.

"Is the intel reliable?" Alpha says.

"We got this," Charlie says.

"We'll discuss it at the brief," the BC says.

"I know," Charlie says, "and you'll want to roll heavy and send Delta, but they're all fucked up, losing men and shit. We haven't lost any Joes. We—"

"We'll discuss it at the fucking brief."

I'm at the top of the stairs, behind Mason in line. We're next to enter the chow hall, but this talk has me turned away, facing Charlie, my rifle pointed right at his face. His eyes are hidden behind sunglasses with slightly bulging black lenses. Below is a very red, very fat mustache—well out of regs. I center my front sight post in the small shadow of his chin dimple, my rear aperture framing a circle around his throat and mouth in my line of sight. My thumb is on my selector switch but I have not rotated it. My finger is resting on my trigger guard. I'm marching to the funeral and the other companies are lined up along the way, all of Charlie is lined up and I'm counting them as I go, I'm counting every soldier in Charlie company as I pass them and I see it in their faces, in every goddamn one, they aren't sympathetic or sorrowful, they aren't reading us as we pass, I'm counting them and they are all there, every last one, not a single casualty, and in their faces I see relief.

"Mills," Mason says quietly, trying to edge himself between my barrel and the stair railing.

We haven't lost any Joes. My thumb is resting on my safety switch.

"Mills."

The BC looks up. "Sergeant Mills?"

"Sir?"

"Can we help you?"

I lower my rifle. "No, sir."

"Delta company, right?"

"Yes, sir."

Charlie looks to his boots.

"Carry on then," the BC says. To the commanders, "I lost my fucking appetite." He walks away toward the TOC.

I stand there, hard-eyeing Charlie. Around his broad mustache, his cheeks are sunburned. His sunglasses glint as he squares his face to me. I like him better over my rifle sights. He says, "BC says carry on, Sergeant."

I go into the chow hall.

"What are you doing?" Mason asks, as we slide past the pizza and the hamburgers.

"What?"

"Were you going to shoot Charlie's Company Commander?"

"Did you hear what he said? Fuck that guy. I wasn't going to shoot him, that's just how I listen to bullshit."

"Uh huh," Mason says. "And how about the rifle?"

My mouth opens, hangs, but I have no answer. Mason sets a plate of noodle salad on my tray. He shuffles down the line. I follow.

"What rifle?" I finally muster.

He smiles at me. "It's okay. It's okay that there was blood in the back of your truck when we ran the numbers. It's okay that you made me search his room so you wouldn't have to. It's okay that you don't want to tell me."

I'm looking into my noodle salad.

"Mills, it's okay. But if you're going to crack up, just let me know, so I can step far enough away that they leave me out of it." He's smiling at me softly.

"It fell. In the fucking dirt. All I wanted to do was save him," I say. "Save it."

"I know," Mason says. "You were right to pick it up. But you still have it. It's now stolen. You stole an M-4. That's, like, prison or something if they catch you. Leavenworth, I don't know. You either send it the fuck home or leave it on Napes's bunk for Kurtzson to find. If you get caught, you're fucked."

VII

Outside the chow hall the heat begins to suck at my energy and I regret throwing away my food again. The line of incoming men wash their hands in the basin of the molded plastic sink station. There are no paper towels, they shake their hands in the hot air and in seconds they're dry. I walk around to the back of the chow hall and in the shade of the trailer I find a pallet of bottled water, stacked as tall as me, with the plastic-wrap holding it together cut down to my chest. I pull out a bottle.

I drink. Even in the shade the water is so warm, drinking it feels worse than the thirst.

Mason knows I have Napes's rifle. He was almost grinning. My stomach drops out and the little bit of water I drank comes back up. I swallow.

I pour water into my palm and smear it across my face. I take off my hat, step out of the shade, and look up. The sun is in the center of the sky. I close my eyes. The water evaporates. I pour water. Spread it over my face. The water evaporates. I do this until Mason comes around the corner.

"Is that helping?" he says.

I put my hat back on. "A little."

"Here." He holds out a hamburger wrapped in foil. "You can fuck around with some things, but food isn't one of them."

I put it inside the cargo-pocket of my pants.

The last bit of water sloshes in the bottle. I drink it. My stomach settles some. "Thanks for the burger," I say. There is a garbage can on the far side of the pallet, overflowing with empty bottles. They are piled up all around, a three-foot tall heap of waste, quietly waiting to be emptied. I throw mine on top. It slides down the side of the pile, just about back to my feet. I nudge it forward with the toe of my boot. Next to the garbage can is a pile of flattened cardboard boxes. I dig through a few until I find one that has all four sides, with no tears in the flaps. I put it under my arm, and walk clear of the garbage. Mason shakes his head.

We cross the road that leads in from the main gate and bisects the small base. We can already hear Kurtzson's voice coming over the motor pool wall.

When we pass the Hesco barriers, Kurtzson is lighting into Hicks behind my truck. My arm tenses around the box. Hicks is sweating. Spit's flying from Kurtzson's mouth.

To me, Mason says, "Yeah, I'm not watching this shit show." He slaps my shoulder. "And eat that fucking burger." He heads inside.

Hicks says, "We lost it taking fire. It's fucking gone."

One meter from the door, standing in the gravel and dust, I am fifteen meters away from their spit and sweat. The sun looks down squarely on the three of us. They are nose to nose. Kurtzson leans in, tightens up, begins to speak. The door next to me bangs open and two Joes blow past, on their way to chow. They are laughing. The door bangs closed behind them. When I turn back, Hicks and Kurtzson are looking at me.

Fuck.

"Sergeant Mills," Kurtzson says, "come here." Warm water sits at the base of my throat. I'm breathing through my nose, trying to swallow it down. Hicks takes a step back, but stays facing Kurtzson.

"Sergeant?" I say, walking over.

"Napes's rifle," Kurtzson says. I'm sweating through my blouse, into the box under my arm. "It's still missing."

"It fell off the truck when we took fire," I say. Hicks nods tightly.

"No shit," Kurtzson says. "Nobody's contesting that." He takes a step forward. He towers over me, looking down, his face dark in the shade of his hat. His ears and neck are burned red. I think I hear the blood pulsing in the artery coming out of his collar. Maybe it's just my own. "You're the dismount, right? Why didn't you pick the fucking thing up?"

I don't look away. In my periphery Hicks's head drops forward, eyes toward the ground. "I didn't see it," I say.

"So you take fire from a single shooter and suddenly forget how to soldier, and go running for your fucking truck?"

"No, Sergeant."

"You did. You lost your shit, you went pussy or retarded, I'll let you pick."

"Napes was shot. The command was to mount up. That's what I did."

"Bullshit. Went pussy."

"Maybe I did," I say. "This war business is scary."

Kurtzson grabs me by my collar with both fists, pulls them together, slowly pinching off my blood supply. His nose is touching mine. There's warm water and bile taste in my mouth.

"Take your fucking hands off him," Hicks says, putting a hand on each of us, trying to pry us apart.

"Last fucking chance," Kurtzson says. "Did you see a rifle fall off that truck?"

One hand squeezes my pistol grip, the other holds the edge of my box. The pressure around my neck makes the edges of my vision light up, flashes and sparks. I raise my chin, stretch out my neck until the lights die out. "No, Sergeant."

Kurtzson looks back and forth at us, resting his eyes on Hicks. He pushes me hard, it takes me three strides to catch myself. I take two steps forward. He reaches his index finger to the center of my chest, drags it across to my shoulder, and taps the flattened cardboard: *tick tick tick.*

"Bullshit," he says.

Inside my room, I lean my rifle against my bunk and drop the box onto the floor. I push out the sides and tape the bottom together. I take the hamburger out of my pocket, unwrap the foil, and take a bite. My guts spasm a little. I swallow. Nothing moves. I take another bite. I chew. I set the wrapper on my bed and the burger on top. I pull the two halves of Napes's rifle from behind my books. I take a bite. I wrap each receiver in a towel and place them inside the box. I shake it a little. I take a bite. I take soft cover books off my bookshelf and wedge them between the rolled towels. I shake it again. Better. I eat the last of the burger. I tape the top closed. I throw the foil in the garbage. I set the box on my lap. I hold it there. I expect my stomach to turn, but it doesn't, it just sits with me, quietly, like the box.

When I lift the box between my hands it's heavy. Heavier than when it was only a rifle. I close my eyes and imagine Nicole opening our front door, signing for the box, setting it on the dining room table, dragging the pearl-handled serrated knife we only use for opening mail along its taped edges, pulling apart the flaps, and instead of scarves or paper weights or pieces of shrapnel or Republican Guard-era bayonets or his and hers matching fake Rolexes or money with Saddam's face on it, when she pulls apart the flaps and unrolls the towels a fucking rifle falls out and that's when she'll know, she will already have heard about Napes, but at that moment, when the rifle falls to the floor, she'll know that it happened, that Napes got killed and I lost my shit, at the clank on the floor she'll know that I broke.

I address the box to home.

VIII

There are five soldiers in line ahead of me. Five behind me.
    Heavy mail day.
    "Next," she says. Her uniform is crisp.
    The box is weightless in my hands.
    Four ahead. Five behind.
    The screen door opens, lets the sun fall in.
    "Next," she says.
    Three ahead. Six behind.
    I shake the box. Feels empty.
    Sunlight from the door.
    "Next."
    Two ahead. Seven behind.
    Eight behind.
    Sunlight.
    Kurtzson enters.
    "Next," she says.
    One ahead. Nine behind.
    Kurtzson behind.
    This box was heavy yesterday.
    Weightless now.
    "Next."
    Sunlight.

IX

Mason says Leavenworth. Kurtzson put his hands on me—he wants to do more than paperwork. Sawyer is out again, bed left made. I wonder if he's talked to Kurtzson, if he's seen anything worth reporting. I put my rifle under my sleeping bag. I cut open the box, slicing my address in half, and pull out Napes's rifle. As my hands move, it starts coming apart. I lay it out on my bunk so that no piece is hidden. There are so many pieces. One at a time, I lift them, roll the small ones between my fingers, slippery with CLP. The longer ones I pass from hand to hand. I close my eyes. I'm searching.

There's a knock at the door. I look across the bunk. When I'm sure I can't make out the outline of my rifle beneath Napes's parts and my sleeping bag, I say, "Come in."

Gleeson enters, sits on Sawyer's bunk. He looks like all of us, red-eyed and swollen-faced. He looks at the rifle pieces. "Is it helping?"

"I think so."

"That's good." In his hands is a book. He's turning it over, again and again. "I need to do something repetitive too."

"Are you reading another Thompson?"

Gleeson holds it out to me. *Fight Club*. "He said it was his favorite book. Kept trying to get me to read it. I don't know why I wouldn't. Anyway, after Alvarez, I definitely wasn't going to, you know, because it was something he wanted, to share this thing with me. And I was just so goddamn mad at him." He is staring at the cover of the book. "But I went to check, you know, just hoping it was still there. Kurtzson was packing up his stuff. It was just sitting there. He said he loved it, that I had to read it. I just took it." Gleeson is letting the pages slip past his thumb. It makes a quiet whirring sound. He does it over and over. He presses harder. It makes a short *zip* sound.

I turn back to the pieces. I pick up the firing pin. I hold

it in my fist. It's like squeezing a small bone. It's about as long as my hand is wide, its large end like the head of a nail, tapering away toward the end that sets bullets to their task. It's perfect. Gleeson is looking at his book. *Zip*. I put Napes's firing pin inside the left breast pocket of my blouse. It slides narrow-end first and doesn't fall sideways. I feel it through the shirtfront, still metal within, but softer now.

I reassemble the rifle. "You need a box? It's a good box. Whatever you put inside goes weightless. It will save you loads on shipping."

Gleeson stops turning the book. "No, I'm good."

My stomach growls so loud we both look to my middle. "Chow?"

"I'm not hungry." *Zip*.

X

The alarm on my watch wakes me. Three o'clock in the morning. I put on my pants and blouse. Sawyer is snoring in his bunk. I sling Napes's rifle, the strap over my left shoulder, the butt of the rifle sitting in the crook of my right armpit, and shuffle barefoot out into the hall. From around the corner I hear the fake laughs of an old TV show crackling out of laptop speakers. Whoever is on shift in the company TOC is watching but not laughing.

I take a bottle of water out of the hallway freezer and walk to the latrine. I swish freezing cold water in my mouth and spit into the sink. I pour it into my hands and wash my face. My whiskers are days old. I drink from the bottle. I piss.

In the room where the junior enlisted sleep, I remove the sling from Napes's rifle, roll it tightly around the two metal strap-keepers, and secure it in my cargo pocket. I come to the first bunk. Gleeson. A book is poking out from under his pillow. I crouch next to him, twist hard, and release the carrying handle and iron sights from Napes's M-4. I push its coolness into Gleeson's sleeping hand. He starts awake. "What the fuck?"

"Shhh." I lean in close. "This is a piece of Napes's rifle. Take care of it. Mail it home or bury it in your platoon box. But take care of it. You get his sights."

Gleeson is blinking. His hand squeezes around mine and the piece of metal. I squeeze back, then pull my hand free. "And I'm taking this." I slip *Fight Club* under my arm. "Napes was what he was. No different than any of us. But a kid. He fucked up and got Alvarez killed. He was going to have to carry that." Gleeson reaches up, thumbs the edge of the book, his eyes glossy in the dim light, tears building at the corners. "We put him in that turret, you and me. But somebody was going to die up there. And any of us still might. These aren't the gravy days—we're still in the shit. Learn to live with it later."

He lets go of the book, pulls the handle to the center of his chest, and rolls his back to me, face to the wall. "Thank you," he says.

At the next bunk, I set the book on Burnside's sleeping chest, my hand on top, and shake gently until both his hands are over mine, him looking up at me. "Shhh," I say. "Gleeson thought you'd like to have it. He was borrowing it from Napes." He turns it over, smiles. "He'll wish he'd been up there the rest of his life. You can stop telling him now. He knows. He'll know forever." I give him the charging handle. "This is a piece of Napes's rifle. Take care of it."

He looks at what's in his hands. "Thank you."

I move from bunk to bunk, lightening my load. One bunk gets the upper fore grip. The lower fore grip goes to the next. Then the buffer. The buffer spring. Cold metal into warm hands. "Shhh," I say. "Take care of it."

"I will."

"I promise."

"Thank you."

The long room is dark. Small orange and green and blue lights glow from electric clock-faces. Most of the platoon is now awake, lying silent.

I get to Mason. I have three pieces left in my hands, the upper and lower receivers, and the bolt assembly. When he wakes he's up and at me before I can shush him. His fists are at my shirt collar, pulling down. The choke comes on fast and he holds it until he says, "Mills?" He releases his grip. "You scared the shit out of me."

I rub my throat, swallow a couple times, catch my breath. "I have something for you." I hold out the bolt assembly. He looks at it. Slowly, he takes it. He turns it over in his hands.

"What happened to mailing it home?"

"I don't need it gone, I need help carrying it."

I wake up to Sawyer standing over me. "What the fuck?" he says.

I sit up, shake my head, look at my watch. Eight o'clock.

"You've had it this whole time?" He's standing close, his leg is touching my bed frame.

I find the half-full water bottle by my feet and drink long and slow. "I don't have it anymore."

"No shit." He sits down beside me. His jaw is working and his chin is loose. He's trying to keep his face together.

"You going to report me?"

He picks up my bottle, twists off the cap, and spits dark spit into it. "I should. I fucking should." He sets the bottle down. His eyes are all twitch and water. "Kurtzson asked about it. I said I hadn't seen anything. I have no idea why you think I'm the asshole here, what the fuck did I do?"

I can't stand Sawyer because he's better at this than I am, because he's here and he's on missions and he's at the hotels and he still makes up his bunk every goddamn day, because I think he might be made for this shit and I don't want anyone to be made for this. But my chest contracts and I think I hear a cracking sound coming from inside me. "Nothing," I say. "You did nothing." I reach down and pull out the lower receiver from under my bunk, the buffer and buffer spring already gone. "I wasn't sure if you wanted it."

"Of course I fucking want it." He tucks it under his arm and spits into the bottle again.

"Send it home." I nod to the empty box next to my bookshelf. "Take care of it."

"Thanks." He wraps the receiver in a towel from his laundry bag, packs them into the box, and goes out.

"Enter," Hicks says. He's sitting on his bunk facing the door. A book in his hands.

"Sergeant, do you have a minute?"

"Sure, Sergeant Mills." He sets his book down.

I sit in the only chair in the room. My rifle is hanging down my front and I have a full laundry bag in my lap. "I wanted you to know that I washed my sheets." I reach into the bag and pull out Napes's upper receiver. I set it across the MRE box he uses as a nightstand. We both stare at it. He says nothing. "I washed my sheets. All cleaned up." The receiver is stripped of grips and carrying handle. The guts have been removed. Hicks blinks dryly, slowly putting together a smile.

"Glad to hear it, Sergeant Mills. Glad to hear it." He picks up the receiver and pushes it under his green wool blanket, its silhouette under the black-printed U.S. next to where he's sitting. "Thanks for letting me know."

"Roger, I'll go make up my bunk now."

I pull my sleeping bag onto the floor and spread my clean sheet over my mattress. I tuck in the overhang, I pinch out hospital corners.

I retrieve a plastic bag from the bottom of my duffle bag and replace it with my sleeping bag. Inside the plastic bag is a desert uniform, cleaned and pressed, that I've never worn. I thought it would be nice to wear a perfect uniform on the flight home. I think it's a better idea to wear it today.

It's mid-afternoon and the shower water is air temperature. I soap and shampoo and brush my teeth and floss and see my browning face in the mirror and see hair starting to touch my ears and when I pull the uniform on the starch sounds like cardboard against my skin. I trace the lines of creases down my legs and arms. I tuck my pant legs into my boots and my dogtags beneath my undershirt.

Walking back from dinner chow with Mason, the sun is nowhere near setting. The breeze comes up over the perimeter walls and smells like riverbank. For the first time in a week I cleaned my plate and don't feel like puking.

"Good chow," Mason says.

"It feels good to eat." The door to the barbershop beside the laundry is still open. "I'll meet up with you later."

The barber, young and Iraqi, waves me into the chair. He shears the back and sides of my head down to nothing. Fades the top into a high-and-tight. The lather on the nape of my neck is warm. He drags the straight razor down and away. Rinses it in a bowl of perfumed water. It comes out clean. Drag and rinse. I close my eyes. He smells of sweat, strong tea, and rose flower oil. I breathe deep.

He runs a finger down my jaw line. "You need shave."

I feel my face, it's days' worth of growth. "Okay."

Warm lather. The drag and rinse. Drag and rinse. He towels me roughly and powders my neck. I come out clean.

I push an American twenty into his hand. "Shukran," I say.

He gives me a hug. My raw cheek is pressed against his, he is warm, soft. I don't mean to but I squeeze too hard. He's softer than my pistol grip, won't leave rigid impressions pressed into my skin when I let go, and his arms are around me, squeezing back, he just stands, lets me hold on to him for all I'm worth, I squeeze and he squeezes back and when I do finally let go, when he sees my tears, he just smiles.

I reach out another twenty toward him.

He kisses me on the cheek, leaves the money in my hand.

Kurtzson is in the motor pool when I come around the Hesco barriers. He's watching Gleeson and Burnside police garbage from around the trucks. "Hurry the fuck up. At this rate, you'll miss chow altogether." Gleeson sees me. He tries to look away fast but his face squeezes in around his eyes and he mouths the word *fuck*. Kurtzson looks over. "Sergeant Mills, just in time." Burnside drops a cigarette butt into the black plastic bag he's carrying.

I walk over, stop when I'm flush with the headlight. "Sergeant?"

"Police call," Kurtzson says.

"So I see." He's standing at the front tire, leaning over the hood of my humvee, eating a piece of pie from a paper plate with a plastic fork. He has a speck of brown filling on his chin. "How long has this been going on?" He's two bites away from reaching the crust.

"A while," he says. "Trying to jog some memories." He forks a bite. There's filling at the edges of his chewing mouth.

Gleeson and Burnside bending and grabbing and throwing away. The rustle of the plastic bag like leaves.

Kurtzson smiles but hasn't finished chewing.

"Men," I say, "go get chow. I need to talk to Sergeant Kurtzson. Alone." Kurtzson takes another bite. Chews thoroughly. Runs his tongue over his teeth. Sucks at them. Smiles big with them. The filling is still on his chin. Crust on his plate. He sets his fork down and Gleeson and Burnside are gone.

"You have something to tell me?"

"Yes, Sergeant." I reach into my starched cargo-pocket and pull out the rolled strap from Napes's rifle. I set the black coil on the hood between us.

"What the fuck is that?"

"That is what's left of Napes's rifle." I dig back into my

cargo pocket. I drop the two strap-keepers onto the hood. *Tink tink.*

The bottom edge of the sun is level with the perimeter wall. Soon the sky will be orange, then red, then black. Kurtzson stares at the strap.

"I found it on top of the turret the day he died—no rifle attached," I say.

"I found it buried in the back of the truck when we got back," I say.

"I found it on the dirty street when I was running to the truck," I say.

"I found it poking out of Napes's body-bag when he was lying dead in the medics' room," I say.

"I found it attached to his rifle after it slid off the back of the humvee," I say. "This is the only piece I didn't mail home."

"This is the only piece I didn't mail to Napes's parents, on account of the soaked-up blood," I say.

"I picked it up and dispersed its pieces to every man in the platoon," I say.

"This is the last piece of Napes's rifle. I thought you should have it."

Kurtzson isn't smiling. He picks up his fork, jams it into his crust. Two tines break. He keeps trying. "That will be all, Sergeant Mills. Get out of my fucking sight."

I make it halfway to the barracks door before I turn to look. He is buttoning his cargo pocket—the strap is gone from the hood. "Sergeant Kurtzson," I say, "take care of it."

He doesn't say anything. Wind picks up dust, drags it across the motor pool between us. There is wind.

I reach up to my breast pocket, find the bone-feel of Napes's firing pin under crisp uniform, and squeeze.

ACKNOWLEDGMENTS

Thank you to the journals and anthologies that original-
ly published earlier pieces of *The Horse Latitudes*, including
Split Lip Magazine, *Gobshite Quarterly*, *Nailed Magazine*,
O-Dark-Thirty, *War Stories 2015: an anthology* (Blue Skirt
Press), *Clackamas Literary Review*, and *The Road Ahead*
(Pegasus Books).

Love and gratitude to my family and friends.

And to the "Volunteers" of 2/162 Infantry Battalion.
Yes, even the brass.

Love and thanks to my workshop, without whom
I would never finish stories: Marina Callahan, Nikki
Levine, Thea Prieto, and Steph Wong Ken.

Thanks to everyone in my MFA cohort at Portland
State University for meeting early drafts of this book
with kindness. And thank you to the faculty who have
instructed me, then and now: Diana Abu-Jaber, Charles
D'Ambrosio, Michele Glazer, and Nam Le.

And to John Larison at Oregon State University for telling me to keep going, and for telling me that MFAs were a thing.

Thank you to my early readers: Brandon Hubbard, Liz Prato, Edie Rylander, Davis Slater, Valerie Wagner, and all of the Foul Weather Writers.

To Nicole Campbell, thank you for telling me to write, years before I thought I could. And for the kids. That was a good goddamn idea.

I have two green army men on my desk:

To Lidia Yuknavitch, thank you for telling me, over a not very good story, that I could work harder, and for calling me a writer. You were the first. And thank you for your support ever since.

To Leni Zumas, thank you for making me want to be better, for being an exceptional writer and teacher, and for saying yes only when the words weren't shitty. Thank you, my friend.

And to Dan DeWeese. Thank you for your instruction, your writing, your editing, your feedback, and your support. And for taking this very small thing that I had to write in order to keep going, and giving it a home with Propeller Books.

PROPELLER BOOKS

THE HORSE LATITUDES
BY MATTHEW ROBINSON
2016

TRANS EUROPE EXPRESS
BY ELIZABETH LOPEMAN
2014

THE PARABLE OF YOU
BY TONY WOLK
2013

DISORDER
BY DAN DEWEESE
2012

A SIMPLE MACHINE, LIKE THE LEVER
BY EVAN P. SCHNEIDER
2011

NINE SIMPLE PATTERNS FOR
COMPLICATED WOMEN
BY MARY RECHNER
2010